THE MASKED MAN

Throughout the history of the Wild West, many men chose to hide their features beneath a mask whilst riding as outlaws, but there was only one man who rode on the side of law and order and yet wore a raised black bandanna over his face. Riding to the aid of those who could not defend themselves against the evil that spread across the ranges, Clu McCall concealed his face from those who had harmed and still threatened his loved ones. So it was that McCall became the one man all outlaws feared – the famed Masked Man.

THE MASKED MAN

THE MASKED MAN

by

Michael D. George

Dales Large Print Books
Long Preston, North Yorkshire,
BD23 4ND, England.

British Library Cataloguing in Publication Data.

George, Michael D.
    The masked man.

    A catalogue record of this book is
    available from the British Library

    ISBN   1-84262-349-4 pbk

First published in Great Britain 2003 by Robert Hale Limited

Copyright © Michael D. George 2003

Cover illustration © Longarron by arrangement with
Norma Editorial S.A.

Published in Large Print 2004 by arrangement with
Robert Hale Ltd.

Dales Large Print is an imprint of Library Magna Books Ltd.

Printed and bound in Great Britain by
T.J. (International) Ltd., Cornwall, PL28 8RW

Dedicated to the memory of Buck Jones.
A true hero.

ONE

During the history of what has become known as the Wild West, many men hid their true identities from knowing eyes, behind the slender protection of a mask. Most of these men were ruthless outlaws, but not all.

There was one man who rode on the side of law and order even though he wore a black bandanna over his lower face pulled up to just below his eyes.

A man who struck terror into the black hearts of those who had sold their souls to the Devil himself.

The rider who wore the black mask had once been a famed lawman and only chose to disguise himself in order to protect those who were close to him. A man who had seen his entire family destroyed by evil and vowed to never allow that to happen to anybody else whilst there was still breath in his body.

The mask enabled him to give those who were left of his friends a little bit of protection. For even they had no idea who it was behind the raised black mask. That was their protection.

He had seen what revenge looked like when it was administered with deadly weaponry by those who killed without a second thought or hint of conscience. It was the only way that he could continue to fight on the side of the law.

To be always unrecognizable and never allow anyone to get close enough to see the real man behind the disguise was not easy. It called for a man of immense inner strength. A man who would never be honoured for his bravery and daring. Yet this was his way, it was the only way.

This was a price he was willing to accept and pay.

His fame had grown quickly amongst those who feared him. He had ridden alone for nearly five years since adopting his simple but effective disguise. Keeping true to his personal vow; always to protect those who were not capable of protecting themselves.

Never seeking or accepting the praise or thanks that his valiant actions richly deserved, he rode on, knowing that whilst he lived no one would kill innocent people the way that his own family had been murdered. It was impossible to bring them back to life, but the husbands, wives and children of others could sleep easily in their beds at night when he was in the saddle.

He did what had to be done.

There was no one else either willing or capable. He was alone and that had become the way he liked it. He was utterly fearless in his pursuit of justice. It drove him on and on. It seemed that nothing frightened the tall rider clad entirely in black as he appeared in one town after another like a phantom.

Appearing and disappearing, seemingly at will.

It seemed impossible that anyone who looked as distinctive as he could find out so much about those who feared him as he somehow did.

But there was nothing mystical about him. He simply used, the one ploy that nobody had ever thought about, to enable him to get as close as possible to the enemies of law, order and justice. He would simply shed his black clothes and mask and hide his magnificent white horse on the outskirts of town and then dress like an ordinary cowboy and ride in on his second horse, a brown mare.

He became just another drifting rider amongst so many others in a land full of aimless cowboys. By showing his face, he found that he could make himself virtually invisible.

There had been more than a hundred towns over the years that had not given Clu McCall a second look. In each town he had used a different name, but no one ever remembered them or even seeing him.

Allowing his beard to grow or changing the accent of his voice added even more confusion to those around him.

There had been times when he even dared to take jobs as deputies to confound even more those who were his sworn enemies. Again, no one ever remembered what he looked like once he had disappeared and changed into his famed *alter ego.*

The mysterious masked horseman had become known throughout the West by good and bad men alike as someone who could not be intimidated by anyone.

Even the various tribes of Indians, who had learned long ago to be wary of white men, respected the rider who rode straight and true.

Unlike so many others who rode through the West, he was a man who could be trusted.

Someone whose word was his bond.

A master with his pearl-handled Colts and a superb athlete, he had become feared by all those who had ever witnessed him riding his eighteen-hands pure-white Tennessee walking horse.

But no one knew his name.

As he thundered from one lawless town to the next, he was known as, simply, the Masked Man.

TWO

Medicine Lance was a town where conflict was no stranger to any of its citizens. A large sprawling lawless town that seemed to be growing with every passing season, it rested on the sun-baked banks of the Cheyenne River, set neatly between two high snow-topped mountain ranges, fringed by a million trees. A land of brutal contrasts and filled with men of equal ferocity.

A town that was not quite ready to give up its lawless past and embrace a more peaceful future.

Yet there were only two things that had enabled Medicine Lance to exist at all. The first had been the cattle that thrived on the lush grass which covered the rolling hills up to the tree lines as well as the fertile unfenced open ranges to either side of the ice-cold Cheyenne River which cut through them.

The second was a series of trading posts that had been set up across the once-barren plains. These trading posts had brought the luxuries of the distant East to the wilds of the rugged West.

Goods were the lifeblood of all growing places and the trading of these goods kept civilization moving ever westward on its relentless journey in search of the almost mythical California goldfields.

Yet all was not well in or around Medicine Lance. For months tension had been steadily increasing as greed finally raised its ugly head in the fragile community. The men who ruled this land like ancient emperors suddenly began to realize that what they had at first conceived of as merely a small trading post, was actually the most westward part of a vast business empire: a business empire of which they wanted a share.

For ten years one man, who had worked himself harder than most, would drive his hired help in order to establish his chain of trading posts across the once untamed landscape. For that entire decade he had withstood all that nature could throw at him to achieve his dream of having trading posts spanning the entire breadth of America. He had ventured into territories that even the army had not attempted to tame. He had fought sandstorms and blizzards and never once doubted his own destiny.

Jethro Eccleston had a fire in his soul that refused to be extinguished by anything or anyone. He had been thirty-five years of age when he sailed aboard a clipper from Liverpool in England to the shores of the Hudson River.

With barely enough money in his pocket to buy a square meal, he had worked hard and saved. Within ten years he had opened his first store on the bustling streets of New York. Six years later he owned twelve and was already venturing out into the unknown lands that bore little resemblance to anything he had ever encountered before.

Then he had had a vision which would change his entire life. The thought of opening up one trading post after another across the mainly uncharted heartland of America would soon become more than an ambition, it would become an obsession that dominated his entire waking day.

Eccleston would always be there at the head of his ever-growing empire of trading posts, ensuring that each one was up and running before breaking new ground in his quest to create the next.

New trading posts meant new opportunities. Furs of every description were readily traded for everything that had come from the factories back East. Eccleston used his supply trains of heavily stocked wagons to ferry goods back and forth along his chain of trading posts.

Even though he had been forced to change his chosen routes many times because of the unpredictable terrain, Eccleston had forged on and on until he had reached Medicine Lance.

Then, for the first time since he had established his original trading post, he encountered trouble.

At first it just seemed that he was being plagued by a series of unlucky coincidences. Accidents and then attacks on his wagon trains started to halt the progress of his well-oiled machine until supplies in either direction became almost impossible to arrange.

For years Eccleston had hardly needed to use money in any of his trading posts. He had grown wealthy by trading cotton fabrics and farm tools to men who would exchange them for valuable furs and even gold-dust. Refined sugar and salt had brought him the most profit, though, and steadily his bank balance back East had swollen.

Yet now, for the very first time since he had begun to execute his dream, everything was going wrong. He was losing valuable goods to bands of robbers in both directions and this was costing him dearly.

When the trouble had started, the wily Englishman had just thought that fate was finally catching up with him and making him pay for all the generosity it had bestowed upon him over the previous decade.

The Indian attacks on his wagon trains had been thought to just be natural native hostilities at first, but then it became obvious that there was cunning planning behind them. They were not mere coincidences or lucky strikes by the Cheyenne braves who lived in the high trees, but the work of someone who had far more serious motives.

Eccleston had encountered many Indians as he built one trading post after another across the American heartland. Not one of them would plan anything as deliberate as this.

Yet whoever was behind this, it was costing him dearly.

With mounting debts and banks starting to question the financial wisdom of the man who had once been their best customer, Jethro Eccleston began to realize that this was not just a bad phase in his otherwise glittering business career. The truth was far more disturbing: only a white man would want something that badly. The Cheyenne knew nothing of greed.

Someone in Medicine Lance wanted to break Eccleston and take control of the string of trading posts that he had spent so long establishing.

He wondered who this man could be who was so ruthlessly controlling the Indians to do his bidding.

The answer would be revealed far sooner than Jethro Eccleston imagined.

THREE

Medicine Lance seemed to resemble many other towns dotted throughout the West and yet there was a difference that nobody could see. It lay hidden from honest eyes just below the surface of corruption that covered the sprawling town. For the thing that made this town different was the fact that it lay in the fertile valley between two high mountain ranges.

There was a price men had to pay in order to be allowed to settle on its plains or just to pass through on their way to the distant western coast. Faced with finding another route to their destination, men simply paid up.

The man who controlled Medicine Lance had become sole owner of everything within a hundred square miles. The man gave the appearance of being just another cattle rancher like so many others, but in reality he was someone far more dangerous.

Burly Ben Braddock was a man who knew what he wanted and exactly how to get it. He wanted everything and would not hesitate for even a second in sending in his men to destroy all who stood in his way.

Greed controlled this would-be rancher. It always had. The ranges of the once-virgin West had provided him with more wealth than he could have spent in a dozen lifetimes, and yet his appetite was never satisfied.

Braddock had managed to create what became known as Medicine Lance when others feared the tree-covered mountainsides where it was known that at least a thousand Cheyenne still dwelled as they had always done. This had been their ancestral home and even when the buffalo had been driven to near-extinction and no longer made their way through the lush fertile valleys, the Indians remained.

But Braddock had known how to control the Cheyenne, as he had controlled every one else whom he had encountered during his fifty-two years of stealing and cheating.

He provided them with cattle and they did his bidding. The more they complied with his demands, the more they were able to feed their young and old.

The warriors, all 300 of them, soon realized that it paid to let this ugly white creature dictate to them if they wanted to eat well and survive in a world that was changing faster than any of them could comprehend.

More than a score of hired gunfighters had also sold their souls to the large man with the sickly pale skin. These men did exactly as they were told and never once considered disobeying the burly Braddock.

To disobey him was to put your neck on the executioner's block and Braddock wielded vengeance swiftly. No one had ever chanced his arm with this man for he was a man who had nothing except greed flowing in his veins.

Braddock always got what he wanted because he had learned long ago how to control people whatever their colour. The Cheyenne were a very useful addition to his army of followers. They also diverted attention from him.

When he sent the painted warriors on a mission he knew that few would dare point an accusing finger in his direction. It was simply the savages doing what they had always done.

No one was safe from Braddock's insatiable appetite for money and power. He allowed settlers to bring in herds of cattle and then sent in the Cheyenne and his own men to take everything they had off them.

For years he had waited for them to become prosperous and then stripped it from each and every one of them.

Anyone who dared to speak against Braddock, died. There was no other way. For he controlled everyone and everything in and around Medicine Lance.

He was the vital source of wealth that sustained every man, woman and child within the boundaries of Medicine Lance. Like blood-sucking leeches, they all fed off the money that the large cattleman had managed to accumulate.

There were no contenders for his throne for none of the people who lived in or around the township knew how you could defeat such an enemy. Most were satisfied with their lot, knowing that they would probably be worse off if he were deposed from his powerful position.

Ben Braddock had managed to convince even those who hated him that he was the answer to their dreams. He knew how to manipulate people's minds like a master puppeteer and relished the feeling he got from doing just that.

He was the undisputed ruler of this land.

Yet always he wanted more and more. For greed never truly dies in the black hearts of men who, like Braddock, seem unable to have quite enough money or power. He had enough of both to last him another hundred years of living and yet it was not enough.

There could never be enough.

Ben Braddock had noticed the trading post on the outskirts of Medicine Lance, and seen how much business it was doing. So much business that his curiosity was aroused into finding out more about it and the strange man who had built it.

He soon discovered that Jethro Eccleston was no ordinary storekeeper, as he had at first assumed. The man with the strange accent was no mere storekeeper, but the sole owner of a company that stretched all the way back to the distant eastern seaboard.

When Braddock had dug even deeper for information about Eccleston he was shocked to discover how wealthy the man really was. He had a company that was worth hundreds of thousands of dollars. Eccleston was ripe and ready for picking.

Braddock knew then that he would have to try to gain control of the company somehow. He knew that he alone could accomplish this feat because only he had the power.

Unlike other property that he had seized by sheer brute force this string of trading posts was legally owned by Jethro Eccleston. A slightly different strategy would be called for.

It would take every ounce of the brutal cunning that he had honed to perfection over more than fifty years to bring Eccleston down to his knees.

But there was nobody more qualified in this profession than Ben Braddock.

He always got what he wanted.

FOUR

No one gave the unarmed cowboy a second look as the brown mare ambled out of the heat haze toward the trading post. There were already a few horses tied up outside the building made from trimmed pine-trees. As the rider pulled the horse to a halt next to the crowded hitching rail, he looked up at the man he knew to be Jethro Eccleston.

Clu McCall knew that he was taking a gamble in discarding his famed pistols and the disguise that put fear into all who looked upon it, but he had to try to find out what was happening to the recently built trading post. To do that, he had to try to appear like just another drifting cowboy.

Simply while leaning against a bar in Medicine Lance he had already learned that this man named Eccleston had the strangest of accents anyone in these parts had ever heard.

It was true.

As Eccleston talked to one of his customers who was leaving the trading post with his purchases, the cowboy tried to work out whether the man was actually speaking the same language as everyone else.

Eccleston watched the man mount and ride back in the direction of Medicine Lance before he even noticed Clu McCall sliding off his saddle.

'Can I help you, son?'

Clu McCall had allowed his whiskers to grow for a few days and had pulled the front of his hair down so that it dangled over his face from beneath the battered hat. He climbed the three steps until he was standing next to the trading-post owner.

'I reckon so, partner.'

'What are you looking for?' Eccleston enquired.

'Some new chaps.' McCall replied sheepishly. 'I plumb worn the last 'uns out on a trail drive.'

Eccleston beamed. 'You have come to the right place. We have some dandy new chaps inside, son. Leather or woollies? Which'll it be?'

McCall shrugged and tried to maintain the stoop he knew would make him appear far shorter than his true height.

'Leather, I reckon,' McCall drawled slowly. 'I ain't partial to sheep at the best of times.'

Eccleston held out his hand in the direction of the open doorway.

'It's all in here, son. Come and take yourself a look. What we ain't got, I can order for you from our catalogue. We can get you anything that your heart desires from our catalogue.'

Clu McCall shuffled into the cool interior of the trading post and gazed around it. He had never seen so many items for sale under one roof.

'Do you have liquor?'

Eccleston laughed as he made his way past

his other customers until he was back at the long counter.

'That is the one thing that I do not stock, my friend. There are enough saloons in the town yonder to satisfy a thirsty man. I just sell goods. I got some soda pop if you're real thirsty though.'

'Soda pop?' McCall shook his head. 'Nope. I ain't that thirsty.'

Eccleston supervised his youthful assistant as they saw to the other customers, while McCall sat himself down on an upturned barrel of nails. He listened to the strange accent as the man served the other men until they left the trading post laden down with goods. He still could not understand more than every other word that came out of Eccleston's mouth.

The sun was low and red beams traced in through the three windows. It was nearly the end of another blisteringly hot day, but McCall knew that this was when the most danger seemed to occur in these parts.

'You want fancy chaps or just honest

working-man ones?' came the question from the trading post man.

Clu McCall rubbed his mouth.

'Just normal cowboy chaps, mister. I ain't no dude.'

'Right. I have three designs. I'll get them for you to have a look at.'

Clu McCall watched as the young man who obviously worked for Eccleston lit a series of oil-lanterns which were dotted around the interior of the trading post.

The entire building seemed to be bathed in an orange glow as the sun finally set behind one of the mountain ranges opposite the trading post.

McCall had heard about the strange Indian raids that had become almost a nightly ritual. They seemed to have only one target: the trading post. Yet so far the raids had only destroyed outbuildings and property belonging to the Englishman but not wounded anyone.

Not yet.

It just did not add up in the mind of the

man who was known as the Masked Man. He knew a lot of Indians throughout the wild untamed West and had never known any of them to attack simply for the fun of it.

Jethro Eccleston returned from the back of the store with three pairs of heavy leather chaps over his arm. He stood directly in front of the seemingly shy cowboy and started talking about them in turn. McCall pretended to be listening to the sales talk whilst really studying the entire store around him.

It was difficult to get a true sense of the size of the place due to its being filled with every manner of trading goods.

'Something troubling you, son?' Eccleston asked as he began to realize that McCall's mind seemed to be on something else. 'You don't seem too interested in these chaps at all.'

'You get much trouble around here?' McCall asked in a tone that was designed not to alarm the man.

Jethro Eccleston stopped talking for a moment and looked down on the crumpled figure sitting before him. He had no idea who this man truly was but knew he was not what he pretended to be.

'Why would you ask a question like that, son?'

McCall shrugged and reached out. His fingers rubbed the leather chaps closest to him as if they were inspecting the quality of the garment.

'No reason. I just heard tell that some pesky Indians have been causing you some grief.'

Eccleston turned to the young man who was working behind the long counter, stacking boxes.

'You can go home now, Danny. I'll close up. See you in the morning.'

'Thank you kindly, Mr E.' The young man named Danny did not have to be told twice. He grabbed his coat and hat and scurried out of the door. A few moments later the sound of the youngster's horse could be heard heading off towards town.

'You ain't answered my question, *amigo.*' Clu McCall said quietly as he watched the man.

Eccleston walked away from his customer and laid the three pairs of chaps over the counter. He said nothing until he had made his way around it.

'Who are you, stranger?' The question was asked at the same moment as his thumb pulled the hammers back on a well-oiled scattergun.

A scattergun which was aimed straight at McCall.

McCall tilted his head and stared across the distance between them into the twin barrels of the cocked weapon.

'I don't understand.'

The scattergun was held in hands that refused to shake.

'You ain't no cowboy looking to buy chaps. So who and what are you really?' Jethro Eccleston growled.

Clu McCall considered standing but knew

that to do so was dangerous when a double-barrelled shotgun was aimed at you no more than twelve feet away. He remained seated.

'You're as smart as folks say you are. I've fooled a lot of people with this disguise but you seen through me like I was a window-pane.'

Eccleston lifted the wooden stock of the weapon more firmly to his shoulder and repeated his question.

'I asked you who and what you are, stranger. I want an answer or I'll let you taste both barrels.'

McCall swallowed hard.

'My name is of no matter.'

'OK. We'll skip your name. That still don't make me any the clearer as to what you are. Are you a gunslinger? A hired gun sent to finish me off after those fake Indian raids?'

'No gunslinger, Mr Eccleston.' McCall said as he considered the man's words carefully. 'What do you mean by fake Indian raids?'

Eccleston walked back from behind his counter. He kept the deadly twin barrels trained on the seated man with every step that he took.

'I might be from back East but I can tell the difference between real Indians and fake ones. I know that the last raid which burned down my supply shack was the work of both,' he said.

Clu McCall sat upright and looked at Eccleston through the limp strands of his hair covering most of his face.

'You mean that white men were riding with Indians?'

'Yes. That's exactly what I mean. Unless the Cheyenne warriors have suddenly started to grow moustaches and side whiskers, then white men were riding with Indians.'

'This sure don't add up right,' Clu McCall muttered under his breath.

Eccleston took a step closer.

'You're making me nervous. I want some answers fast.'

The man dressed as a simple cowboy could see that Eccleston's hands were now starting to shake. That was never a good omen for someone holding a weapon renowned for having hair triggers.

'Don't get too close. It ain't healthy for innocent folks to know what I look like. That's why I usually wear a mask,' McCall said calmly.

'So you're an outlaw?'

'Nope. I am here to help you.'

'I don't hire saddle tramps.'

'Have you ever heard of the Masked Man?'

Eccleston squinted at the man before him through the lantern-light. For the first time he realized that there was enough hair and grime covering the features of the cowboy to make it impossible to know what he actually looked like.

'I've heard of him. Why?'

'I'm the Masked Man. I'm here to offer you some help.'

'Why would you want to help me?'

McCall turned his head as he heard the sound of riders approaching. An awful lot of riders.

'It sounds like you have uninvited guests,

Mr Eccleston.'

'They're coming again!'

'Give me a carbine and I'll help you fend them off.'

'How do I know I can trust you?' Eccleston asked. 'You might be one of them.'

Clu McCall rose to his full height.

'Trust me.'

For some reason the owner of the trading post lowered his scattergun and indicated to the wall behind the counter. McCall looked and saw the dozen or more brand-new repeating rifles lined up on a shelf.

'I hope I don't live to regret this. Help yourself.'

McCall leapt over the counter with the agility of a puma and grabbed a Winchester. He looked through the stacked boxes of rifle shells until he found the correct ones, then bounded back to the side of the terrified Eccleston.

'Blow out them lanterns otherwise we'll be sitting ducks in here,' McCall ordered as his experienced fingers speedily slid one bullet after another into the rifle's magazine.

The trading-post owner did exactly as he was told. For the first time in twenty years he was actually taking orders from someone else. Yet he did not argue. This was not the sort of business of which he had any real knowledge.

This was obviously the forte of the man loading the Winchester frantically beside the open doorway.

When the light from the last lantern was extinguished both men stood shoulder to shoulder staring out into the darkness.

The sound of thundering hoofs grew louder with every passing tick of the wall clock behind them.

'What are you going to do?' Eccleston whispered.

McCall cranked the mechanism of the rifle. He did not reply.

FIVE

From out of the darkness the scores of painted ponies swarmed like hornets around the solitary remaining building of those that had once formed the trading-post compound.

A hundred or more war cries filled the night air as the horses began to circle the isolated building. Clu McCall raised the rifle to his shoulder and stroked its trigger with his index finger. His keen blue eyes studied the riders as best as they could in the eerie light of the moon.

There were indeed more than a hundred of them in full battledress riding around the trading post. McCall noted the rifles carried by several of the Cheyenne. They were not the usual single-shot Springfields that most Indians used – rifles that had been salvaged from battles with soldiers over the years. These were the gleaming barrels of Winchester repeating rifles.

The only thing that gave McCall any hope was that most of the screaming riders seemed to be armed with only bows and arrows. He knew that however accurate an Indian was with his bow, whilst riding bareback he could not compete with the lethal venom of a carbine.

McCall pulled his companion back behind his own wide shoulders and continued to stare down the length of the rifle in his hands at the riders. Most of the riders had braided their hair, but at least ten per cent of them had war bonnets on their heads.

That seemed too many.

Then it occurred to McCall that it was highly unusual for any of the Plains Indians to attack after sundown. Yet these Indians were doing just that.

Could Jethro Eccleston be correct in his assumption that some of these Cheyenne braves were in fact white men?

Moonlight danced off the tips of the arrows as they sprang from the Cheyenne bows and hurtled towards the building where McCall and Eccleston were trapped.

McCall jumped backwards as the door was skewered with the deadly shafts of a volley of Cheyenne arrows.

He could see that his brown mare was terrified as it fought to free itself of the reins that held it secured to the hitching pole outside the besieged trading post.

With deadly accuracy McCall fired one shot at the hitching pole and severed the reins. He watched as his bucking mare galloped through the circling Cheyenne riders.

Suddenly a volley of bullets blasted from the barrels of the Indians' Winchesters.

The doorframe was ripped to shreds beside the two men.

Splinters and sawdust showered over both McCall and Eccleston as the younger man forced the older down on to the floor. He pushed the lever of his rifle down sharply and expelled the casing of his spent bullet from the rifle's magazine.

He hauled the lever back up and fired again.

In the light of the moon he saw one of the riders tumbling off his pony. Yet no sooner had the Indian hit the dusty ground than he was scooped up by another of the Cheyenne.

The war cries grew louder and louder.

'We've had it, son,' Eccleston said from his enforced hiding-place.

'We ain't dead yet,' McCall said, cocking his rifle again and firing at the passing horsemen. 'It ain't over 'til the fat lady sings.'

Before Eccleston could speak again a terrifying sound chilled him to his marrow. It sounded like a hundred rattlers flying through the air.

Then both men knew what the sound was.

Every glass pane in the entire building was shattered as dozens of arrows came in at them from all sides. A million fragments of glass rained on the pair as arrows embedded themselves into everything around them.

McCall had dropped on to one knee as splinters of glass fell over him from the closest window. An arrow vibrated next to his right arm as it came to rest in a large packing-case.

'It's a good job you got a lot of stock in here, Mr E.' Clu McCall shouted above the sound of the cries of the warriors outside the trading post. 'Otherwise we would have been riddled with arrows by now.'

'I sure hope they don't start using fire arrows like they did on the store shed.' Eccleston gulped.

McCall cranked the rifle again.

'They ain't intending to burn this building down.'

'How can you be so sure?'

'Easy.' McCall fired again. 'Otherwise they'd have done it by now.'

Eccleston was not convinced. Sweat was pouring down his face like rainwater. He had travelled nearly half-way across this great land without ever coming up against such hostility as this.

'What do they want? What do the bastards want?'

'They seem to want you to get kinda spooked.' McCall patted the man's shoulder, then rose to his full height and stepped out of the door on to the wooden boardwalk.

Without a second thought for his own safety, McCall began to fire the rifle faster than any of the Cheyenne warriors had ever seen anyone do. His shots were not aimed to kill but to let the horsemen know that he could kill if he so chose.

He blasted the rifles and bows from the hands of every rider at whom he aimed. Clouds of dust rose into the air as the Cheyenne pulled back on their crude rawhide reins and stopped their advancing mounts.

McCall fired at the feathered war bonnets and sent feathers billowing into the air above the riders.

Suddenly he realized that the bone-chilling war cries had stopped and the Indians were lined up before him.

His keen eyes darted across the faces of

the riders. He vainly searched for faces that were not Cheyenne. If there were white men amongst this bunch, he thought, they were at the back of the hundred or so Indians.

With a courage few men could equal, he stepped down from the boardwalk and walked to within a dozen feet of the horsemen.

His blue eyes stared at the almost elaborately dressed Indian who sat astride a painted pinto.

The two men looked at each other for more than a minute as if reading each other's minds. Then the Cheyenne chief raised his bow above his head and turned his pony.

Clu McCall began to breathe again as he watched the riders disappearing in the cloud of dust kicked up off the hoofs of their mounts.

Jethro Eccleston staggered out from the trading post in a state of total shock. He walked across the moonlit ground until he was next to the silent man.

'You scared the critters off, son.'

McCall lowered the rifle and shook his head.

'Nope. They weren't scared, they were just humbled.'

'What do you mean?' Eccleston asked.

McCall placed a couple of fingers in his mouth and whistled loud enough to make the older man cringe.

'There ain't no honour for a Cheyenne to kill an unarmed man.'

Eccleston grabbed the rifle from McCall.

'What do you mean, unarmed? What's this if it ain't a rifle?'

'It's empty and their chief knew it,' McCall replied as he saw his brown mare galloping out of the brush towards him.

Jethro Eccleston pointed the barrel at the ground and squeezed its trigger. The rifle was indeed empty.

'You faced them Indians with an empty Winchester?'

McCall grabbed the reins of the mare and threw himself on to his saddle. He turned the mount and stared at the dust which led to the high tree-covered mountainside.

'You gotta know how the Cheyenne think. They're the most fearsome fighters there are, but they won't kill a fellow warrior in cold blood.'

'You took a big risk. I reckon you must be the Masked Man just like you said you were.'

McCall turned the mount and rode off towards the opposite line of trees. He had to reach his hidden camp and change into the famed Masked Man once more. There was a lot of work to be done before this night was over.

SIX

The morning sun had not yet reached its zenith but that did not make it any the less hot. Three hours earlier Clu McCall had changed into his black clothes and tied the bandanna across his face to disguise his features. Then he had ridden away from his hiding-place high in the wooded mountainside east of Medicine Lance.

He had ridden for all he was worth to the one place that he knew might provide him with some answers to the countless questions that burned in his craw.

Stirrup, the white stallion, had eaten up the ground beneath its hoofs as its long legs thundered in the direction in which its master was steering it. No other horse could have covered so much ground in so little time as the Tennessee walking horse. There was simply no finer or more powerful mount anywhere in the wilds of the West and McCall knew it.

Coming up over a sandy ridge, the rider pulled back on his reins at the sight before him. Yet he did not stop, but drove the horse on at even greater speed. The fiery mount did not falter for one second as it galloped down towards its distant goal.

Fort Waverley spanned more than fifty acres and had stood unchallenged ever since it had been first constructed on the vast open range which had once been filled with migrating buffalo.

Few ventured anywhere near the remote garrison any longer except the rider who knew the post well and was known to the entire 500 souls who lived within its high wooden walls.

The Masked Man hauled in the reins of the strong white horse and allowed it to walk slowly over the last twenty or so yards to the open gates.

The sentries in the twin towers to either

side of the gates looked down on the unmistakable figure and waved their rifle barrels in greeting to him.

The Masked Man touched the brim of his Stetson in reply.

'Howdy, boys,' he called out. 'Inform Colonel Walker that the Masked Man has come visiting.'

One of the sentries called down to a trooper who went scurrying off in the direction of the whitewashed buildings.

'What brings ya back here, Masked Man?' the other sentry called down from his tower to the rider clad entirely in black.

Clu McCall teased back on his reins and stopped the horse just below the towers. He pushed his Stetson back off his damp brow.

'I've come to have a word with the colonel, Sam.'

The sentry gestured to the rider.

'Head on in, Masked Man. You know where to go.'

'I ought to. I've been here enough times, Sam.' The rider tapped his spurs against the sides of his horse and rode on through the gateway and across the enormous parade ground. He did know the layout of the garrison well. Clu McCall had been here many times, both as himself and as the Masked Man.

Over the years one building after another had sprouted up in the huge compound of Fort Waverley until it was almost a small town. McCall rode the barely sweating mount towards the array of adobe buildings until he saw the familiar figure of Colonel Zack Walker stepping out from his office into the blazing morning sun.

The distinguished officer had a mane of white hair flowing over the collar of his dark-blue tunic and a well-clipped beard to match. It seemed to McCall that he had never seen the man without an unlit cigar gripped between his teeth.

Walker smiled as he rested his shoulder against a wooden upright. For some reason the two men had built up a bond of trust between them over the years.

'Good to see you, Masked Man.'

'It's mutual, Colonel,' McCall drawled.

'I got me a feeling that there must be trouble out there someplace for you to turn up here unannounced,' Walker said. 'You never bring good news nowadays.'

The Masked Man shrugged. 'Reckon you could be right there.'

Walker stared out at the people milling around his massive garrison. He had turned this remote outpost of the 7th Cavalry into a community that was totally self-contained. A place where the troubles of the rest of the world seemed so very far away.

'How long have we known one another?' the colonel asked.

'Quite a while.'

'Seems longer.' Walker smiled.

Clu McCall looped his reins around the hitching pole outside the whitewashed building and then stepped up on the raised boardwalk beside a man whom he had grown to consider his best friend. His blue eyes peered over the top of his bandanna at the hardened cavalry officer.

'There's trouble brewing out there, Zack,' the Masked Man said. 'Real dangerous trouble.'

'Where?'

'As far as I can determine, it's centred in or around Medicine Lance,' McCall answered.

Zack Walker straightened up and ran fingers down his white beard. He knew that if this man was worried, there was indeed something to fret about.

'What sort of trouble?'

'Somebody is stirring up the Cheyenne and getting them to attack the trading post and its supply wagons.' The Masked Man strode around the colonel and stared out at the fortress compound. There were hundreds of soldiers moving around the huge parade ground, going from building to building. The officers' wives were few in number but their colourful clothes were a welcome contrast to the sun-baked ground which seemed to stretch off in every direction from where

McCall and Walker stood.

'That's mighty interesting,' Walker replied. 'I've had word in dispatches that a number of trading posts and wagon trains have also been attacked over the last couple of months as far away as Fort Bravo.'

The Masked Man looked straight at his friend.

'Others?'

'Yep. And they all belong to a character named Jethro Eccleston,' Walker said.

'I've met Eccleston. He's a good man who has been pushed to breaking-point.' Clu McCall rested a gloved hand on an upright. 'Fort Bravo? That's a hundred miles from here.'

'Ninety-one to be exact,' Walker corrected.

McCall raised an eyebrow as he considered the information his friend had just imparted.

'Were they also attacked by Cheyenne?'

'Yep. That's what my dispatches said.' The colonel nodded. 'A whole bunch of the critters. Maybe two hundred or more.'

The Masked Man shook his head slowly.

'It don't make no sense.'

'You're dead right there, son,' Zack Walker agreed. 'It don't make no sense at all.'

McCall could tell that there was more.

'What haven't you told me, Zack?'

'You're sharper than a straight razor.' Walker grinned. 'There is more but it don't clear nothing up. It just makes it even more confusing.'

'What is it?'

Colonel Walker inhaled deeply.

'The strange thing about those Indian raids is that they have not killed anyone yet. The Cheyenne have destroyed livestock and goods, but not one of the wagon drivers has had anything more serious than a few scratches.'

The Masked Man ran the back of his glove across his brow as the words sank in.

'That is odd. Why would they take the risk of attacking so far from their camp and not kill anyone?'

Colonel Walker nodded. 'If they had killed civilians, I'd have been forced to send a couple of hundred troopers after them.'

McCall stretched up to his full height as if suddenly he was beginning to make sense of the information that he had been given.

'Of course, that's it!'

'What?'

Clu McCall squared up to the officer.

'They didn't want anyone killed. That would have brought you down on their necks, Zack.'

'But why would they waste their time attacking the trading posts and their supply trains?' Walker's face showed his utter confusion.

'What if they are being controlled by some-one who simply wants to ruin Eccleston?' the Masked Man asked. 'Someone who knows that if he wants to keep the cavalry out of this, the Cheyenne must be ordered not to kill those wagon drivers.'

'Do you think that a white man is behind all this?'

The Masked Man nodded.

'Damn right, Zack. It has to be a white

man. No Indian would be so devious. Eccleston told me that there were white men riding with those Indians when they attacked his Medicine Lance trading post. I thought he was mistaken.'

'Even so, I can't justify sending troopers into Medicine Lance until someone actually gets killed,' the colonel said regretfully. 'But if you need ammunition, it's yours.'

The Masked Man exhaled loudly.

'Thanks, Zack. Some extra ammunition might come in real useful.'

Walker placed a hand on the younger man's shoulder.

'Only when someone is killed am I free to act.'

McCall's eyes stared into those of his friend.

'By then it might be a tad late. My worry is that whoever is behind the Cheyenne raids is going to start a war.'

'Who do you think could control a couple of hundred Cheyenne warriors so skilfully?' The colonel pulled his cigar from his mouth and stared at the chewed-up object thought-fully.

There was a long pause as the Masked Man stared out at the people who were going about their daily routines inside the fortress compound. 'If I find that out, we'll have our man.'

SEVEN

He was a man who knew that for all his medals and power, he had probably never displayed a fraction of the bravery as had the rider who was heading back to the distant Medicine Lance. For he was tied hand and foot by regulations and sometimes those very regulations could be something to hide behind. An excuse for not doing what you knew needed to be done. For all the years the officer had known the man who hid his features behind the black bandanna, he had never discovered what drove him on and on to risk his own life in the aid of others.

What had happened in this man's life that made him take such a course?

Colonel Zack Walker watched the magnificent white stallion galloping from Fort Waverley with mixed feelings. He knew that the Masked Man was taking on something that neither of them could fully comprehend.

What was going on at the distant Medicine Lance?

Walker wanted to help the Masked Man more than he could ever admit, but knew that if he were to send a platoon of uninvited cavalry troopers into Medicine Lance, he might just provoke the trouble that he was trying to avoid.

There were many people in and around the distant town set between two mountain ranges who would not take kindly to the interference of the cavalry.

Yet what was happening there?

It was just one of countless questions that had traced through the experienced officer's mind. Yet for all his concern, his hands were tied by red tape. There was nothing in his massive rule-book that could cope with this sort of thing, and that angered him.

He knew that the Masked Man was taking on far more than anyone was capable of coping with. There were hundreds of

Cheyenne braves in those mountains ready and more than capable of wiping out entire towns if they wanted to do so. Then there were the white leaders of the area who controlled everything that went on there.

Colonel Walker pondered. Was it possible for the Masked Man to overcome such odds alone?

His eyes looked up at the pair of officers who were coming towards him from the direction of the parade ground. One was Robert Cooper and the other, Sidney Tremain. Both were captains fresh out of West Point Military Academy and both still wet behind their ears.

Zack Walker removed the long unlit cigar from his lips and pointed it at the two men. He raised his voice.

'Get me General Hastings at Fort Bravo on the telegraph, Captain Cooper,' Walker ordered loudly waving the cigar. 'You can help him, Captain Tremain.'

The two young officers gritted their teeth as they stepped up on to the shaded boardwalk outside Walker's quarters. Both men glanced at one another before licking their lips and facing Walker.

Robert Cooper removed his hat and looked at his commanding officer. He cleared his throat.

'What's wrong, Cooper?' Walker asked.

'The wires are down, sir,' Cooper informed him.

'The wires are down?' The colonel repeated the statement in disbelief.

'Yes, sir,' Tremain confirmed. 'That is correct.'

Zack Walker crushed the cigar in his hand and glared at the young men before him. He knew the value of the telegraph link to other fortresses.

'Why was I not informed about this, Captain?'

'It was only discovered early this morning and I informed Major Stone. He has taken a troop and is riding east trying to find the break in the wires,' Cooper replied sheepishly.

Colonel Walker sighed. 'Major Stone knew of this and yet did not see fit to tell me? He then decides to take out a troop of men without permission?'

'Yes, sir,' Tremain bit his lip.

Walker nodded angrily.

'That's just dandy!'

'I thought you knew.' Captain Cooper shrugged.

'No, Captain, I did not know.' Walker watched as the tobacco leaves fell from his hand to the boardwalk. 'Stone has been a thorn in my side since he arrived here. He thinks that sitting behind a desk has given him the experience to look after men out there.'

The two young officers stepped down on to the parade ground and stood in the midday sun, waiting for the brooding man to speak again.

To their surprise, he did not. Colonel Walker turned and strode into the cool interior of his quarters and slammed the door behind him.

EIGHT

The land east of Fort Waverley was arid. The grass was burned brown beneath the merciless sun and stretched off for ever over the rolling hills. Patches of brush and a few areas of withered trees were the only landmarks that surrounded the riders as they rode into the deep gully. The patrol of ten cavalry troopers had followed the line of telegraph poles for more than ten miles when their sharp-eyed officer spotted the pair of severed wires hanging limply from the high wooden cross-bar of the fifteen-foot-high pole.

Major John Stone had drawn in his reins and stopped his nine followers at the base of the pole. The elegant man dismounted and dusted the trail grime from his tunic as his troopers gathered around him.

Stone had only been at Fort Waverley for six weeks and had earned the bars on his shoulders while sitting at a desk far to the east of this hostile landscape. It was the first time he had ever been in charge of any details and he wanted to impress his superior, Zack Walker.

The officer stood beside his mount and drank freely from his canteen as a burly sergeant-major named Bronsky gave the troopers their instructions.

Eventually, as he saw the men gathering at the foot of the tall telegraph pole, Stone decided to impart his renowned gems of wisdom to the dust-caked soldiers.

'I think that we ought to make camp here and proceed with the repairs in the morning,' Stone said arrogantly.

The nine cavalrymen all turned their faces and looked at the officer, who seemed more concerned with his uniform than completing the job they had been sent out to do.

Bronsky had never quite understood men who used perfume on their uniforms in an attempt to cover the tell-tale signs of human aromas. The big man marched over the rough ground and stopped beside the unconcerned major.

'Did I hear ya right, Major?' Bronsky growled like a bear with a sore head.

Stone glanced briefly at the huge man whose uniform had probably never truly fitted that massive frame since the day it was first issued.

'Are you deaf as well as filthy, Sergeant?'

Bronsky inhaled deeply and felt himself straightening up to his full six feet three inches of height. He glared through narrowed eyes down at the smaller man, who looked as if he were trying to become a picture in an army manual.

'I reckon the major ain't too used to this sort of land or he would not have said what he just said.'

Stone waved a hand at the sergeant as if trying to will him away.

'My orders are quite straightforward. We make camp and then, in the morning, we shall repair the telegraph wire.'

'That ain't right. We gotta fix them wires now.' Bronsky leaned down over the man. His eyes burned into the face that still seemed incapable of understanding anything about this unforgiving place.

'There is no hurry.'

'The army post needs them wires fixed now,' Bronsky repeated. 'I am gonna send them boys up that pole and make sure that they fix them right now.'

'I think not,' Stone responded. 'I give the orders around here. Not you.'

'But them telegraph wires are vital to the security of Fort Waverley Major,' Bronsky insisted.

'Vital? Nothing ever happens in this damn awful country. They can wait.' Stone walked away and faced the troopers who were taking their equipment off the backs of their pack-mules. 'You men can stop that right now and get my tent erected.'

'But we can't be more than ten miles from the fort. What the hell are we making camp for?' Bronsky's voice boomed at the officer.

'You heard me, men.' Stone pointed at the eight men. 'Erect my tent right now.'

The confused troopers placed all their tools on to the ground and stared in disbelief at their officer, who was studying the land around them.

'Major Stone?' Bronsky said, trying to get the full attention of the man who did not seem to be able to grasp the urgency of their mission. 'With respect I must insist that we get them wires repaired and then head on back to Fort Waverley. This land ain't as peaceful as it appears. The bones of thousands of men lie scattered all around here.'

'I see no bones,' the major snapped.

'Maybe if you had ever had to fight Cheyenne warriors like some of us had to in the past, you might know what I'm talking about.' Bronsky snorted.

'You are starting to annoy me, Bronsky.' Stone sighed as he tapped his chin with the index finger of his right gauntlet.

'I've been on hundreds and hundreds of

these missions over the years, sir,' Bronsky insisted. 'You gotta get ya priorities right or folks can get themselves hurt. Our top priority is fixing the telegraph wires.'

'That's it.' Major Stone turned and pointed straight at the doughty sergeant-major. 'Consider yourself on a charge, mister.'

Bronsky raised both his bushy eyebrows.

'I'm on a charge?'

'Damn right, mister.'

'What for?'

'Undermining the orders of an officer,' Stone snapped. Then he gestured to two of the troopers. 'I want this man restrained, men. Shackle him. I'll see that when we do get back to the fort, those stripes on your sleeves will be removed.'

The troopers gasped.

'You must be plumb loco!' Bronsky shouted.

'Find some shackles and chain up the loud-mouthed oaf.' Stone turned and looked down at some brush with a couple of undernourished trees sprouting out of it. 'I do believe that there might be enough water down there for me to have a bath.'

'If you dig a hundred-foot-deep hole, you wouldn't find enough water to fill a thimble,' Bronsky laughed.

'Do as I have ordered, men.' The major gestured to the stunned troopers.

Sergeant Bronsky moved away from the fearful troopers who had been ordered to chain him up. He lifted the telegraph wires up off the ground and waved them at Stone.

'Look at the ends of these wires, Major.'

Stone ignored the rantings.

'Major!' Bronsky yelled at the top of his deep voice. This time the man turned. His face was almost crimson as he walked up to the stalwart soldier.

'You dare raise your voice to me?'

Bronsky rammed the ends of the wires under the nose of the officer and shouted again.

'Look at them, you halfwit. These wires have been cut through with wire cutters. That means that someone around here don't want the fort knowing something real important. Think, man. Think.'

Major Stone barely glanced at the wires. He simply signalled to the troopers around them.

'They look as if they snapped to me, Bronsky. I cannot stand cowardice. Chain this man up, men.'

Before any of the troubled soldiers could move a muscle and respond to the orders of their inexperienced commanding officer, a chilling noise filled their ears. The men all looked around as a volley of arrows rained in on them.

Hideous screams came from some of the troopers.

Stone seemed to be frozen to the spot as he saw the deadly arrows cutting down the men all around him. The sturdy figure of Sergeant Bronsky buckled as an arrow hit him in his chest. He staggered and fell on to one knee and tried to work out where their attackers were.

Unlike the totally inept Stone, Bronsky

had been involved in many hostile actions during his long army career. With gritted teeth he grabbed at the arm of the standing major and pulled him off his feet. The officer fell heavily at the side of the wounded sergeant as Bronsky tore the arrow from his chest and angrily tossed it aside.

'I told ya that this place was dangerous!' Bronsky mumbled as he tried to plug his bleeding wound with his yellow bandanna.

More arrows flew in from the brush around them and caught three of the remaining troopers, who were trying desperately to get their Springfield rifles from their cavalry saddles.

Bronsky pushed the face of the startled officer hard with the palm of his large hand. Stone fell on his back as the bleeding sergeant pulled out his army-issue revolver and started to return fire.

'Will you snap out of it, Major!' Bronsky screamed at the man who was lying wide-eyed next to him.

'What's happening?' Stone finally managed

to ask.

Bronsky heard the cries of a man who had tasted the venom of one of his bullets as he squeezed the trigger again.

'Ambush!' Bronsky yelled, firing again into the brush from where he had seen the last volley of arrows coming. 'You led us into a damn ambush, you dumb bastard.'

Stone rolled over on to his belly and fumbled for his own pistol. Then he saw more arrows flying high above them before falling at last into the heart of the small group of troopers.

The last of the patrol's uninjured soldiers gave out a pitiful cry, then fell backwards over the major and his growling sergeant-major.

This was no normal fight, this was slaughter.

John Stone's eyes darted around them as even more arrows sped towards them. He was trying to see how many of his small troop were left.

The truth was brutal.

Only he and Bronsky remained.

Pulling back the hammer of his pistol until it locked, the officer tried to control his shaking hand and aim at their unseen enemy.

'Is it Cheyenne?' Stone asked Bronsky.

'Shut up and fire that hogleg, Major,' the big man snapped as he felt his tunic front becoming soaked in his own blood. 'Just shoot at that brush and pray that you hit some of them before they finish us off.'

Both men fired their guns again.

Then, to their right they heard even more arrows being launched into the hot afternoon air. Stone and Bronsky tried to turn around and find cover from the new attack, but there was none.

Deadly arrows came down over the horses and themselves. Stone felt an agonizing pain tearing through both his legs as they were skewered by two of the missiles.

Then the chilling sound of their cavalry mounts filled the air as half of them were hit. The crazed animals galloped off in all directions, some wounded and some just terrified by the smell of warm blood.

Stone rolled back and forth as pain tore through him. He fired his pistol at both the sites from where he had seen the arrows coming before reaching down and grabbing at the two wooden shafts in his legs. One was stuck in the calf of his left leg, having pierced his highly polished leather riding-boot. The other arrow was driven deep into his right thigh. Both were bleeding badly.

'I'm sorry, Bronsky.' Stone apologized to the burly man beside him.

There was no answer.

Major Stone suddenly looked at the motionless figure and held on to the muscular arm. He pulled it and Bronsky rolled over on to his broad back. The arrow in his throat had ended the life of the army veteran.

Suddenly Stone heard noises. They were all around him.

Arrows came at him from all sides. He saw them all as they found his outstretched body.

Then he too followed the nine enlisted men into a place from where there was no return or escape.

The entire massacre had taken only two minutes to complete.

The sound of horses' hoofs echoed around the silent place where the lifeless bodies of the small patrol lay in pools of their own blood. Ben Braddock led the dozen horsemen from their hiding-places and rode at the head of his disguised hired killers. Each of them was dressed in Cheyenne clothing and carried bows.

Braddock stared down at the bodies and laughed louder than any of his followers had ever heard him laugh before.

'That'll put the fox in the hen-house, boys,' he roared as he spurred his mount over the lifeless troopers. 'Now we gotta get back to Medicine Lance. By the time they send out another troop looking for these critters, we'll have finished our business with old Jethro Eccleston and there won't be a single finger aimed in our direction.'

The riders galloped off, knowing that for now it would not be they who would get the blame for this outrage. It would be the Cheyenne, high in the mountains above Medicine Lance.

They would pay the price.

NINE

Dan Weston had ridden with Ben Braddock's bunch of hired gunmen for nearly three years. He was a keen shot and feared nothing either human or animal. Sober, Weston was a force to be reckoned with and he knew it. He earned top wages from Braddock and had become his right-hand man. The trouble with Weston, though, was that he was seldom sober after sundown.

He earned big and drank to match. He had poured more whiskey down his throat over the last decade than all of Braddock's other hired gunfighters put together.

Until now, it had not been a problem.

But, until now, the mysterious Masked Man had not been around.

Weston had left the side of the burly Braddock after they had slaughtered the troop of cavalrymen and headed back for town. He had a thirst on him and it had to be quenched.

Yet the gunfighter knew that he could not ride into Medicine Lance wearing the crude clothing that he and the rest of Braddock's men had worn to ambush the troopers. He had to ride to the remote line shack set amid the trees above Medicine Lance and change back into his own clothes.

Weston drew back on his reins and slid from the saddleless mount. He pulled the moth-eaten Cheyenne blanket off the lathered-up horse and tossed it outside the door of the line shack. He entered and pulled off the soiled clothing and then found his own neatly folded outfit beside those of Braddock and the other riders' shirts and pants.

Weston had not had a drink since setting out at dawn with the ruthless Ben Braddock and he was starting to get the shakes. He knew that only whiskey could stop those shakes and he hurriedly dressed again in his own clothes. He strapped the gunbelt around his middle, fastened the silver buckle and leaned down to tie the leather laces around his broad thighs.

He had never changed his clothing so quickly in all the times that he had ridden on the raids with the Cheyenne alongside his wealthy leader.

Weston slammed the door shut and knew that Braddock and the rest of the gunmen would not reach this place for at least another two hours. By that time he would be well and truly oiled with rye.

He placed his Stetson on his head and tightened the drawstring until it was up under his chin. Then Weston moved to the brush beside the shack and hauled out his saddle and horse blanket.

It took the thirsty man a mere couple of precious minutes of wasted drinking-time to get his horse ready.

Weston mounted and hauled his grey gelding hard around. He started to make his way through the dense tree line towards the high cliff that lay to the west of the mountain range.

Even though he was thirsty for hard liquor, he still obeyed Braddock's rules of using the trail, which would not allow prying eyes to locate the line shack and discover the secrets that lay within it.

The tall trees were so close together above the high cliff that they barely allowed a horse to pass through to the trail that led down to the town below.

Dan Weston allowed his mount to find its own route on the gradual descent that led to the top of the cliff. As he teased the grey on with the tips of his razor-sharp spurs he spotted something that made him haul back on his reins.

The grey came to a sudden stop as it felt the bit in its mouth pulled sharply back. Weston sat silently in his saddle and stared hard at the man dressed entirely in black.

Weston had heard tell many times of this man who rode with the black bandanna tied around his face. For a few moments he wondered whether this was the real Masked Man or simply someone who chose to dress in a similar fashion.

Then he saw the magnificent white stallion.

Without making a sound, Weston reached down and slid his Winchester out from the scabbard beneath his saddle. Carefully he cranked its mechanism.

The Masked Man stepped into his stirrup and mounted the tall stallion, totally unaware of the rifle that was trained upon him.

As the rider with the black bandanna turned the powerful white horse, a shot rang out. Startled, Stirrup suddenly reared up and kicked his hoofs at the air.

Dan Weston watched as the figure clad all in black fell from his horse and disappeared over the rim of the cliff.

Before the deafening sound of the single rifle shot had stopped echoing, the gun-fighter spurred his mount and cut through the trees until he was at the very edge of the high cliff.

Weston held on tightly to his saddle horn,

leaned over as far as he dared and looked down into the dark abyss below his vantage point.

He began to smile.

The Masked Man was gone.

The laughing gunfighter hauled his reins hard to his right and then spurred the mount hard. The grey responded quickly to its master's command. Weston rode down the narrow trail that skimmed the top of the cliff until he found the open range which led him towards the town of Medicine Lance.

For more than five minutes the Masked Man had hung on to a slippery tree-root which protruded out of the rockface. For all of that time he had been trying vainly to find a foothold that would enable him to climb his way back to safety.

He was dangling helplessly at least fifteen feet below the top of the cliff. His gloved hands were losing their battle with the muddy tree-root.

The Masked Man knew that it was only a matter of minutes before his weight would cause the root to slip through his gloved hands.

Every sinew in his body ached as his blue eyes peered over the top of the black bandanna up at his mount, Stirrup, who was looking down at him.

He began to swing back and forth trying to find something to rest his boots on. With every movement he could see the root starting to fray.

Then the tip of his right pointed cowboy-boot managed to locate a small crevice in the almost sheer wall of rock. He forced the toe of the boot in as far as it would go and felt the screaming muscles in his back and shoulders relax. For the first time since he had found himself falling, he began to think that maybe he just might manage to get out of this scrape alive.

The Masked Man pushed himself upward as his right leg straightened on the small foothold. He released his left hand and grabbed out at a jagged rock a few inches higher.

Somehow he managed to force his gloved fingers into the small gap above the jagged rock. He sucked in his belly, then let go with his other hand and grabbed at another small rock.

His dangling left foot at last found an inch-wide ledge and he pressed his full weight on to it. He tried not to think as he inched his way up the wall of rugged granite.

For more than twenty minutes the Masked Man closed the distance between himself and his watching mount. He could see the long loose reins hanging from Stirrup's bridle as the long neck of the curious horse hung over the cliff edge.

'Stay there, boy. Don't you go wandering,' McCall said quietly as his fingers and toes allowed him to move higher up the cliffside.

Then he rested.

The leather reins were hanging just above his head.

He wondered whether they could hold his weight if he were to grab them with both hands. Then he decided that the only way he would find out was to test them.

Taking a deep breath, the Masked Man released the rock with his right hand and slowly tried to raise it over his head. He had to press his entire body against the cliff as his fingers searched for the elusive reins.

Then he felt them.

Using every remaining ounce of his strength, Clu McCall forced his body upward as he closed his gloved hand around the reins and then looped them around his wrist.

He could feel Stirrup pulling him as the faithful mount tried to raise its neck.

'Don't go getting nervous, Stirrup. Not now,' McCall whispered up to the confused white stallion. 'Back up, boy. Back up. You can do it, boy. Pull me up.'

The magnificent white horse began to obey his commands. Stirrup started walking backwards, away from the edge of the cliff. With every step he took, the Masked Man felt himself being raised closer to safety.

His eyes stared hard at the reins.

Would they hold?

Did they have the strength to take his weight?

As he felt himself being hoisted away from danger, McCall grappled with the rockface. His free hand grabbed at every rock, however small, whilst his feet tried to find anything solid enough to stand upon.

He could no longer see his horse.

He was a mere foot or so from the top of the cliff and yet McCall knew that if the reins snapped, he would certainly be unable to stop himself from falling to his death.

'Keep going, Stirrup,' he urged.

Then suddenly the white stallion must have found enough grip beneath his hoofs to take two large backward steps.

The Masked Man found himself being hauled up over the lip of the cliff top with one huge jolt. Lying on his face he began to breathe again. The horse continued pulling until all of McCall's exhausted frame was safe on the sweet grass.

He let go of the reins and then got up on

to his knees. He crawled to his mount, then staggered to his feet beside the white horse.

'You did good, Stirrup.' He panted as he rested his brow against the horse's neck. 'But next time somebody shoots at us, don't buck me off, huh?'

Stirrup began to snort and nod his elegant head up and down as if answering his master.

McCall grabbed the saddle horn and then mounted. He turned the stallion and headed up into the trees.

'Reckon that varmint thinks I'm dead,' McCall muttered through the bandanna as he headed for his secret camp. 'That might just come in useful.'

TEN

Dan Weston had been drinking steadily at the Red Dog saloon for nearly an hour. He had an appetite for whiskey that few, if any, men could equal. Yet for the first time since any of the other regular patrons of the saloon could recall, he was actually smiling. He had seen the famed law enforcer known only as the Masked Man tumbling off the back of his white stallion and falling off the high cliff.

No man could have survived that fall, Weston had repeatedly told himself. There simply was no way a man could plunge nearly 300 feet and live.

Dan Weston had done the impossible.

He had achieved something that no other lawbreaker had ever managed to do.

He had killed the Masked Man.

Weston poured himself another three fingers of rye from the half-empty bottle and tossed it into his mouth. The fiery liquor barely touched the sides of his throat as it burned its way down into his stomach.

The bartender could hardly believe the change in the normally vicious Weston. Yet he, like everyone else within the walls of the Red Dog, was not complaining. As far as they were concerned, this was the most peaceful day in the history of the saloon since Ben Braddock's top gun had chosen to pay it daily visits.

By the time Dan Weston eventually heard the dozen or so riders pulling their mounts to a halt outside in the street, he was as drunk as he could get.

Placing his empty whiskey-glass down on the bar counter, Weston made his way through the busy bar toward the bright sunlight that still blazed down on the wooden buildings.

Braddock noticed Weston first as he steadied his mount in front of the hitching rail. Even he had never seen his right-hand looking so pleased with himself.

'Are you OK, Dan?'

The smiling gunfighter swayed and touched the brim of his hat.

'I ain't never been better, Ben,' Weston replied as the burly man eased himself off the saddle.

'What the hell are you looking so happy about, Dan?' Braddock asked as he tossed his reins to one of the other men to tie to the hitching rail.

'I figure you owe me a bonus.' Weston grinned.

'How come?'

'I killed the Masked Man.'

'You did what?'

'I killed the Masked Man.'

'Where?'

'Up on the high ridge.' Weston sighed. 'I took him off his saddle with one shot and he fell off the cliff.'

'He's dead?' Braddock rubbed his hands together.

'Yep. Dead.'

Ben Braddock could not conceal his own happiness at the unexpected news.

'Good. I heard a rumour that the varmint was sticking his nose into things around here.'

'Not any more.'

Both men laughed.

ELEVEN

Colonel Zack Walker stood silently next to the line of bodies strewn out on the sun-hardened parade ground. He stared down at the lifeless faces of the men whose bodies had been discovered by the patrol he had sent in search of Major Stone.

Captain Cooper had recovered the arrow-filled remains from the dry gully ten miles east of his fortress and brought them all back.

Walker sighed heavily as his eyes looked down at the sturdy blood-soaked body of Sergeant Bronsky. The colonel had known him for more than twenty years and could not believe that he could have been killed so easily.

He stared at what was left of John Stone but could not feel any pity. Walker knew that if anyone was responsible for this slaughter, it was the opinionated major. A man who had thought he knew everything and yet knew nothing at all. This was his fault because he had taken these men without permission from the garrison commander.

Colonel Walker had seldom showed any emotion after the bloody campaigns of his younger days, until this moment. Now he was angry.

The horrific sight of ten of his best men lying covered in their own dried blood made even his iron stomach turn over. He ran his fingers through his mane of white hair and then turned away from the sickening sight.

Suddenly he recalled the Masked Man.

'They were ambushed by Indians, Colonel,' Captain Cooper said, as he tried to come to terms with the gruesome discovery, news of which he had only just brought back to Fort Waverley. 'I think that those Cheyenne are starting to get real ambitious.'

Walker pulled one of the dozens of arrows from the body of a trooper and studied it with eyes that had grown used to the sights and smells of death. He sniffed the feathered flight and raised an eyebrow.

'This arrow has the flight feathers of the Cheyenne, OK?'

'Exactly.' Cooper nodded.

Walker held the arrow out beneath the nose of the young officer.

'But the Indians over Medicine Lance way do not use glue to stick them to the shaft of the arrow. They split the wood and carefully place the feathers into the wood itself.'

Cooper stepped closer and took the arrow from his superior. He looked at it carefully.

'I don't understand.'

Walker exhaled loudly. 'Neither do I, but I intend trying.'

The streets of Medicine Lance were no different to look at from a thousand others dotted across the vast American heartland and yet all was not as it seemed on the surface. People within the boundaries of this town seemed nervous to the keen eyes of the rider, Clu McCall.

Maybe the people looked uneasy because they knew that high above them, on the mountainside, more than a thousand Cheyenne lived amid the countless trees.

McCall doubted that. It had been a long time since the once-mighty tribe had posed any threat to the sprawling town. These people were wary of something far closer to them than that.

He could feel something in the air around him which warned his honed instincts that there was danger here.

A danger that existed somewhere behind the façade of one of these buildings.

McCall guided the brown mare silently through the maze of unpleasant thorough-fares with an open mind. If the men he sought were here, he would find them eventually.

Dressed the same as he had been when he visited Jethro Eccleston's trading post the previous night, the unarmed McCall knew that he would not receive a second glance from any of Medicine Lance's residents.

That was the way he liked it.

To see but not be seen.

To hear but not be heard.

It was the only way that he could locate those who were stirring up the Cheyenne into attacking the trading posts belonging to Eccleston.

His drab appearance would allow him to move around unnoticed from saloon to saloon until he found what he sought. And what he sought was the weak link in the human chain.

For when many men have been involved in the sort of crimes of which he suspected some people here, there was always one person who could not resist bragging to anyone who was willing to listen.

And McCall was always willing to listen.

He pulled back on the reins of the drab horse and dismounted slowly. The streets were busy with people going about their daily routine. None of them even noticed as he looped his reins around a hitching pole and stepped up outside the Red Dog saloon. He pulled the brim of his weathered Stetson down until little of his face could be viewed.

Rubbing his unshaven face with a gloved hand, McCall glanced up and down the long street. There appeared to be nothing unusual there. Men and women were walking in all directions as they did in all busy towns. A number of solitary riders drifted aimlessly up and down the hot street.

Clu McCall studied the hitching poles which were dotted outside almost every building. There were few mounts tied up to them.

He turned and placed his gloved right hand on the swing-doors and pushed his way into the stale-smelling saloon.

The sound of a tinny piano filled the long narrow room drowning out the various conversations of the patrons who were spread out across the saloon.

This was the third saloon he had entered in the past hour and it seemed little different from the others. The bar-girls were reasonably young here, as they had been in the other drinking-holes. That meant that there was money in Medicine Lance. Only towns with money had bar-girls who were attractive.

McCall walked with a slight stoop as he made his way across the sawdust-covered floor towards the long bar. His blue eyes darted from one side to the other with every step. He studied the thirty or so people in the large room carefully.

'What'll it be?' the bartender asked McCall when he reached the long wooden counter.

'A beer,' McCall answered, tossing a silver dollar on to its wet surface.

The bartender picked up the dollar and tested it with his teeth before dropping it into the open drawer of the cash-register. He watched as the man scooped out his change and then placed a glass beneath the beer tap.

'You one of Braddock's new boys?' the man asked McCall as he placed the glass and coins in front of him.

Clu McCall scooped up the coins and slipped them into his vest pocket before lifting the beer-glass to his mouth.

'Maybe,' he replied as his curiosity was awakened.

'You only just missed Ben and his boys. They left for the ranch no more than an hour back.' The bartender sighed and looked out across the quiet room. It seemed that only the girls were doing any business as they led clients up the carpeted staircase for fifteen minutes of pleasure.

'I'll catch up with them.'

'They was celebrating.'

McCall leaned over the bar. 'Celebrating what?'

'Dan Weston kept saying that he'd killed the Masked Man.'

'Who is this Dan Weston critter?'

'He's Ben Braddock's top gun.'

'You want a beer, barkeep?' McCall asked. 'Or maybe we could share a bottle of whiskey?'

'You paying?'

'Yep.'

The bartender beamed. 'Then you got yourself a drinking partner.'

McCall watched as the man lifted a bottle of whiskey off the shelf behind him and blew the dust from it. Unlike the rest of the whiskey-bottles on display in the Red Dog, this one had a good label.

Both men moved to the end of the bar and leaned on opposite sides of its mahogany top. McCall placed two more silver dollars in the outstretched palm.

'Tell me more about Ben Braddock.'

The bartender quickly grabbed the coins and rammed them into his pocket as he pulled the cork from the neck of the whiskey bottle.

'OK, stranger.'

TWELVE

Darkness had fallen swiftly across the lush valley that separated the two mountain ranges. But even the night could not stop Ben Braddock and his dozen or more followers from doing what they had been planning for the last few weeks.

He had to act before the army repaired all the telegraph wires he and his men had cut in every direction leading to the imposing Fort Waverley. There was no way the burly cattleman was going to run the risk of the cavalry being alerted, if he was going to accomplish what he had planned for the next day or two.

Jethro Eccleston had a business empire that stretched off to the eastern seaboard and probably had more money than Braddock had ever dreamed of. He had to keep the man completely cut off from the rest of his company for his plan to work.

Braddock knew how to make men think exactly what he wanted them to think. Eccleston was no different from all the other men he had swindled over the years.

He was just a lot wealthier.

It sounded like thunder rolling through the valley as Braddock led his gunmen eastward along the Cheyenne River toward Medicine Lance and the isolated trading post beyond.

Yet this night there were no disguises.

Braddock knew that he had to show his hand to the man known as Jethro Eccleston. He had to let him see who it was behind the raids on his chain of trading posts without actually admitting to knowing anything about the atrocities.

Yet few were as good at lying through their teeth. For lying was like cheating and stealing. They were things of which Braddock had become an acknowledged master.

It was something that ordinary men would

have found impossible to do, but the burly cattleman was no ordinary man.

Braddock stood in his stirrups and rode at the head of his men with an eagerness that defied most men's logic. He had more than most could ever hope to honestly accumulate in a dozen lifetimes. And he had not made a single penny honestly.

He had learned long ago that the honesty of most men kept them poor and if you wanted to become truly rich, and had no actual skills, you had to become dishonest.

Braddock had become supremely dis-honest.

The riders galloped across the lush fertile range towards the place that they knew was now ripe for harvesting. They had used the Cheyenne braves to put the fear of God into the stranger from back East. They had disrupted his supply of goods in both directions just long enough to make Eccleston wonder whether being in the trading post business was smart.

As the riders whipped their mounts with

their long reins and drove on through Medicine Lance, a hundred onlookers watched with a mixture of fear and admiration. Only one man knew that he had to act and act quickly if they were who he thought they were.

'Is that who I think it is, barkeep?' McCall asked his swaying and belching companion.

'That's Ben Braddock, stranger,' the bartender said, sucking the last of the whiskey from the bottle he had shared with Clu McCall. A bottle, the contents of which McCall had not actually consumed one drop.

'The big man on the chestnut?' McCall asked the bartender, who could barely stand.

'Yep. That's him.'

'I'll remember that horse when I meet its master.'

'But I thought you knew Ben Braddock already?'

'Not until now, barkeep. Not until now.'

Clu McCall stepped down from the

boardwalk outside the Red Dog saloon and untied his reins from the hitching pole. He threw himself on to the saddle of the brown mare and spurred his way along the narrow side-streets until he had nothing but the open range between himself and the tree-covered mountain range.

Glancing over his shoulder at the dust left in the wake of Braddock and his riders, McCall knew that there was little time left. He could not afford to waste a precious second of it.

He could have chased after the riders but he was unarmed and knew that the brown mare had little pace.

McCall forced the horse to gallop beneath the rising moon and a million stars toward the trees. He had a hunch where Braddock was leading his miniature army and what they might do when they got there. He also knew that if he were to have any chance of helping Eccleston, it would have to be as the Masked Man astride his powerful white stallion.

Astride a horse that could cover more ground faster than any other in the territory.

Coyotes howled up in the mountainous crags as was their nightly ritual but McCall paid them no heed. All he could think about was reaching his secret camp and changing into the famed and feared Masked Man.

He knew that once atop Stirrup, he could probably catch up with Ben Braddock.

It would be cutting it mighty fine though.

Yet he had the advantage.

They thought he was dead and nobody fears a dead man.

THIRTEEN

Jethro Eccleston had heard the riders approaching more than five minutes before his ageing eyes were able to make them out in the eerie light of the moon. But this time it was different. Unlike the previous attacks, there were no Indian calls from the Cheyenne or the men he suspected were riding with them.

This night they were riding in silently with only the sound of their horses' hoofs echoing around the massive range to alert the terrified Eccleston of the potential danger that was approaching his trading post.

Fearing for his life, Jethro Eccleston had loaded one of his Winchester rifles long before the sun had disappeared beyond the mountains.

He was ready!

Somehow, he had managed to force himself to venture out on to the small porch and stand watching the moonlit riders heading directly toward him.

Eccleston had never been so afraid.

His finger curled around the trigger of the repeating rifle in readiness. There were at least twelve riders. Even from a quarter of a mile's distance, Eccleston could make out their various Stetson hats illuminated by the bright moon above them in the cloudless sky.

Slowly he cranked the lever on the repeating rifle and held it across his chest. He felt like opening up on them and trying to kill them before they got close enough to kill him but he could not. Every part of his brain screamed at him to start shooting before they reached him, but he began to wonder whether these riders might just be innocent cowboys.

A million doubts began to fill his confused mind.

What if he were to kill them and then

discover they were simply cowboys coming to his trading post just to buy goods or provisions?

Dare he risk it?

For if he did, he would be no better than those who had made his life a misery for the past few weeks. No better, but a whole lot worse.

Sweat began to defy the cool night breeze that drifted off the open range, and started trickling down his weathered face. He was scared and it was an experience that he had never felt before in all the years he had gradually moved across the vast untamed continent.

He was scared of making a mistake.

One that might cost him his life.

Eccleston thought about the stranger who had defended him the previous evening when the Cheyenne had attacked his isolated trading post.

A man who claimed to be the famous Masked Man.

He would know what to do in this

situation, Jethro Eccleston thought.

Sweat ran into his eyes as the terrified man tried to focus on the approaching riders.

With each beat of his pounding heart, they drew closer. The moonlight glinted off the gun grips that jutted from the array of holsters on their hips.

What if they were the men he feared so desperately?

If he were to allow them to just ride up, they might kill him where he was standing.

Up until now, every single raid had been executed by the Indians who dwelled up on the high mountain range. These men were probably a lot of things but they certainly were not Indians, he concluded.

But he was still certain that he had seen some of the so-called Cheyenne warriors with moustaches and side whiskers, and that meant that they could be the driving force behind the series of costly raids.

Eccleston brooded; did it make any sense that now they would show their true colours and identities after spending so much time hiding amongst the Cheyenne warriors?

He swallowed hard.

They were now too close.

Slowly, Eccleston stepped back into the dark interior of his trading post and backed away from the doorway until he could not retreat one step further.

His spine was pressed up against the far wall.

Then he saw the dust as the riders hauled in their reins and stopped their mounts outside the trading post.

Eccleston glanced around the spacious room which was filled with almost every sort of known merchandise. He was thankful that he had been forced to cram his comprehensive stockpile of goods into this building after his store shed had been burned to the ground.

Jethro Eccleston ducked down behind the stacked boxes and began to move deeper into the darkness that only he knew how to negotiate.

'You in there, Eccleston?' the voice of Ben

Braddock called out loudly as the men moved closer to the doorway.

The owner of the trading post tried to swallow.

It was impossible.

FOURTEEN

Ben Braddock and his gunmen cautiously entered the trading post as silently as men with spurs strapped to their boots could. Their guns were drawn and cocked in readiness for trouble. These were men who remembered that Eccleston had been alone the previous night when they had ridden with the Cheyenne.

If the same man was here with Eccleston tonight, they had orders to kill him. And these gunmen would do just that given half a chance for, unlike the noble Cheyenne, they did not respect bravery.

'He's in here, Ben,' Dan Weston said as he held his weapons at waist-level and moved deeper into the dark trading post. 'I can smell him.'

'Stay alert, boys. I wanna talk with

Eccleston, not kill the varmint,' Braddock whispered as he waved his arms and watched the rest of his hired gunfighters fanning out inside the shadowy interior.

Jethro Eccleston knew that he had the advantage in the store which he had single-handedly filled with goods. As long as the uninvited guests did not light any of the lanterns, he could keep out of their way.

'Come out, little man,' Weston taunted as he carefully tried to make his way between the seemingly limitless array of boxes and sacks. 'Come out and talk with us.'

'Ease up, Dan,' Braddock told his right-hand man. 'You'll scare the life out of him before I can discuss business.'

Weston touched the barrel of his Colt against his hat brim in silent obedience.

One of the gunmen whom Braddock had left outside leaned in through the open doorway. His eyes narrowed as he squinted into the half-light. Then he saw the burly figure of his employer.

'He's in here OK, boss. I found his horse

'tied up in the corral out back.'

'Good.' Braddock nodded to the gunman as his eyes stared around the cavernous interior filled almost to the rafters with various goods. There were even ploughs stacked up against the walls amid the sacks and boxes. 'I'd sure hate to be talking to myself.'

A crouching Eccleston tried to reach the far wall but his route was blocked. He knew that he would have to stand upright if he were going to be able to negotiate through the narrow gap. But standing up was the last thing that the man with the Winchester in his sweating hands wanted to do.

Moonlight was filtering through the small glass panes of the windows and Eccleston knew that the eyes of his hunters must have adjusted to the eerie light by now.

He could hear his own staggered breathing and wondered if the men at the opposite end of the trading post might also be able to hear him.

Ben Braddock had given his men strict

orders before they had set out from his ranch. He wanted them to frighten the man even more than they had already managed to do during the raids. He wanted them to hurt Eccleston if that was what it took to get him to agree to signing the legal papers in his inside pocket. But they must not shoot or kill him until those papers were signed.

The burly cattleman moved to the long counter which was barely visible beneath the piles of goods stacked on it. The devious Braddock made his way behind its length as his men tried to fan out in the cluttered interior of the trading post.

'Where are you, Eccleston?' Dan Weston shouted angrily as he stumbled over various sacks and barrels in his search.

'He's in here someplace, boys,' Braddock growled as he reached the end of the long counter and stared into the dark room. 'He must be up the far end. Outflank the swine.'

'Maybe we ought to light a lantern, Ben,' one of his gunmen suggested.

Braddock slammed his fist on the top of

the counter.

'No lights. Not yet.'

Dan Weston cleared his dry throat.

'Damn right. We don't wanna give the bastard too easy a target.'

'Where are you, Eccleston. Show yourself,' Braddock screamed out angrily. 'Are you a coward?'

Jethro Eccleston carefully made his way between the piles of stacked goods as quietly as he was able. But then the long barrel of the Winchester got snagged on a tower of buckets and brought the whole lot clattering down around him.

Eccleston jumped upright and then felt panic overwhelming him as he could see the ten or more faces staring straight at him. He knew that he had given every one of them a target to train their guns upon.

'Don't you move a damn muscle,' Weston said. He kicked his way to the man's side before grabbing the rifle and pushing the cold barrel of his .45 into Eccleston's face. 'I'll kill you if you even blink.'

Braddock struck a match and lit the damp wick of the lantern nearest to him, then lowered the glass bowl. He turned the brass wheel until the orange light filled the room. A smile etched his face as he saw Weston repeatedly jabbing his pistol into the head of Eccleston.

'Dan's got him,' one of the gunman cried, laughing.

'Bring Mr Eccleston here, Dan,' Braddock said in a low calm voice as he found a chair upon which to rest his broad rear.

Before Eccleston reached the long counter where the cattleman waited, he had tasted the blood in his mouth where Dan Weston had tried expertly to break not only his spirit but his teeth.

The owner of the trading post was gasping when at last he reached the counter and rested his shaking hands upon its surface. Blood trickled from the corners of Eccleston's mouth and dripped on to his white shirt-sleeves.

'Do you see what happens when you make

my boys angry, Mr Eccleston?' Ben Braddock coldly asked as his cruel eyes flashed to Weston once more.

The gunman knew what the signal meant. Weston smashed the grip of his gun into the back of the already injured man with as much force as he could muster.

Eccleston gave out a pitiful cry and collapsed.

Braddock nodded again to Weston. The gunman grabbed the thinning hair and hauled their victim back to his feet.

'I hope that I have your full attention.'

Jethro Eccleston was panting like an ancient hound-dog as blood now poured freely from his mouth.

'I'm listening,' he somehow managed to say.

Braddock pulled the legal papers from his inside jacket pocket and unfolded them.

'Sign these papers and we'll leave.'

'I ain't going to sign nothing.'

The cattleman shook his head and sighed.

'I was afraid that you might take that

attitude to doing business with me, Mr Eccleston. I guess you know what's gonna happen now, don't you?'

Before the bleeding man could respond, he felt the barrel of the gun in Weston's hand catching him across the back of his head. It was as if a lightning bolt had exploded inside his skull.

For an instant everything went white as Eccleston felt his head falling forward. He seemed to hear the sound of his temple hitting the top of the counter but was too stunned to feel anything.

Eccleston tried to raise himself off the counter as his eyes cleared but Dan Weston had kicked his legs from beneath him. He landed heavily on the floor.

Although stunned, Eccleston seemed capable of seeing and hearing everything that was going on inside the trading post but incapable of doing anything about it.

'More?' Weston asked Braddock.

The cattleman looked over the edge of the counter at their helpless victim and then up at the gunman.

'I think he can take a little more, Dan.'

As a boot caught him squarely in his ribs, Eccleston could do nothing to protect himself.

He simply had to take the gruesome impact.

And he did.

The kick moved him a good yard to his right. He attempted to scream out but the blood in his throat choked him.

He was almost grateful when he was hauled up again and thrown on to the counter. He had felt as if he were drowning in his own blood when on the floor.

His fingers clawed at the top of the counter as if trying to keep himself from being felled again.

All Eccleston could see was the smiling face of Ben Braddock a mere two feet away from him. He had never seen such a cruel face in all his life. This was a man who took few if any prisoners, he thought.

'Are you ready to sign now, Mr Eccleston?'

'What is that paper?' Eccleston feebly asked, blood dripping from his mouth with every word.

'It makes us equal partners,' Braddock smiled. 'You see I'm not a greedy man. I just want fifty per cent of everything in your business empire.'

Jethro Eccleston shook his head.

'You bastard. Is that what all this has been about? The Indian raids and this? Just to get me to sign over half of what I've spent my entire life creating?'

'Indian raids? What Indian raids?' Braddock grinned. 'I know nothing about Indian raids, Mr Eccleston. I'm just here on business. It seems to me that you could use a partner. Just look at the state of you.'

'I'll never sign that paper.' Eccleston spat blood.

Ben Braddock stared around at the variety of items which surrounded them. There had to be something within these walls would make a useful weapon of torture, he thought.

Then his eyes spotted the ideal thing.

'I got me an idea, boys.' He began to chuckle ruthlessly.

FIFTEEN

The Masked Man thundered out of the trees atop his white stallion and headed straight for the distant lantern-light that spilled from the open doorway of the trading post. It had taken Clu McCall far longer than he had anticipated to reach his secret camp and change himself into the defiant defender of law and order.

With every stride that Stirrup made as he galloped across the lush range, his master knew that all was not right within the walls of the remote log building.

Looking over the top of his black bandanna as he steered the powerful stallion directly at the seemingly deserted building, McCall wondered where Braddock and his cohorts were.

There was no sign of any of the dozen or

so riders whom he had seen heading through Medicine Lance toward Eccleston's trading post a little earlier.

An eerie silence chilled the night air as the Masked Man guided his mount up to the building.

His blue eyes spotted the solitary horse moving nervously around the large corral.

McCall reined in his horse and leaned back against the cantle of his saddle as dust rose from Stirrup's hoofs. He wrapped the long leather reins around the saddle horn and leapt to the ground.

There was a quiet in and around the building that did not sit well with the tall lean man who walked towards it. The light from the lantern within the large log structure flickered across the ground.

For a fleeting moment, McCall considered calling out to the man he knew had to be inside. He dismissed the thought.

Stepping up on to the porch, the Masked Man drew one of his Colts and cocked its hammer before entering.

He did not have to search for Jethro Eccleston.

What was left of the man was lying strapped to one of the large ploughs. There seemed to be blood everywhere as the Masked Man approached the horrific sight. His thumb eased the hammer down on his Colt and slid the unneeded weapon back into its holster.

For a few moments the tall figure just stood silently looking at the man he barely recognized amid the blood.

Exactly what Ben Braddock and his men had done to Eccleston before he had inevitably died, was not clear. All that McCall could tell for certain was that he must have been killed slowly and methodically for some unimaginable reason.

The Masked Man knelt and tried to free the limp blood-soaked body from where it had been left tethered to the honed plough blades.

He had seen many things in his time but had never seen the results of torture before.

McCall lifted the body and then straightened up to his full height. His eyes darted around the large room seeking a place where he might be able to lay what was left of Eccleston to rest with the respect it deserved.

He saw the pile of blankets on top of the long counter and decided that was where he would leave him. Carefully, McCall placed Eccleston on the blankets and then studied the wounds that the man had endured.

McCall still could not believe the sight that his eyes absorbed.

He suddenly felt anger welling up inside him.

Yet it was not just aimed at Braddock, who he knew had to be responsible for this outrage. He was angry with himself for not being here to prevent this.

A thousand thoughts flooded his mind as he wiped the blood from his hands on the end of a blanket.

Why had he wasted so much time in Medicine Lance?

Why had he not anticipated this?

Why did they kill Eccleston?

What had Ben Braddock gained by killing this man?

Then a sound came from the back of the store and alerted Clu McCall that he was not alone as he had assumed.

The Masked Man swung around on his heels. He drew one of his pistols swiftly and aimed it in the direction from where he knew that the noise had come.

For what seemed an eternity, he just stood with the gun held in the hand of his outstretched arm.

'Who's there?' the Masked Man called out.

There was no reply.

McCall knew that it might be one of Braddock's henchmen, left to finish off whoever showed up to help the dead trading post owner.

'Come on out before I start shooting,' McCall warned.

SIXTEEN

A pile of stacked boxes fell noisily to the floor as the shaking figure of Jethro Eccleston's young employee edged his way out of the darkest corner of the trading post to face the mysterious man wearing the black bandanna across his face.

The Masked Man holstered his Colt and watched Danny walking towards him with his arms raised above his head. As the lantern-light lit up the face it was clear that he had shed a lot of tears whilst hiding.

'Lower them arms, son,' McCall said to the frightened youth. 'You ain't got nothing to fear from me. I had nothing to do with this.'

Danny caught a glimpse of Eccleston's body lying on top of the pile of blankets and fell to his knees. His body arched as shock hit him hard.

The Masked Man stepped to the side of the youngster and placed a hand on top of the bushy hair.

'What are you doing here?'

Danny looked up at the eyes that looked over the top of the black bandanna. He did not understand. This man wore a mask and yet seemed to be good whilst the men who had tortured and killed his boss were unmasked.

'Who are you, mister?'

'I'm called the Masked Man,' McCall answered in a low calm voice. 'I ride on the side of law and order and only wear this bandanna to protect the innocent like yourself.'

Danny was still shaking as his fingers clawed at the back of his hand.

'I had finished work but didn't wanna go home. I had me a spat with my pa last night. I went out to my horse and rode off but then returned on foot. I left my horse in the corral and snuck in the back way. I was gonna sleep here tonight.'

'So Eccleston didn't know you were here?'

'No, sir.'

'So that's your horse out there in the corral?' Clu McCall could see how Braddock and his men would have assumed that the horse belonged to Eccleston, just as he himself had done only minutes earlier.

'Mr Eccleston never rode a horse. He drove a buckboard until it was burned in one of the Indian raids and the team was run off,' Danny added.

The Masked Man offered his hand. It was accepted. He helped the shocked youngster to his feet and then led him away from the blood-covered store and out into the fresh air.

'You were here through the whole thing?'

'Yes, sir.' Danny began to shake as he recalled the sounds he had heard as his boss was mercilessly tortured. 'I never heard nothing like it. I didn't know what to do.'

McCall patted Danny's shoulder.

'There was nothing you could have done except maybe ending up like Eccleston.'

135

'Why would Mr Braddock have done that?' There was an innocence in the voice of Danny.

Clu McCall turned the youngster around to face him.

'You saw Ben Braddock?'

'Yes, sir.' Danny nodded. 'I recognized his voice when he was shouting at his men and Mr Eccleston. I peeked out from my hiding-place and saw him as clear as day.'

The Masked Man gave a sigh of satis-faction.

'Do you know what that means? That makes you a witness, son. Now I can make sure that he faces charges.'

The face of the youngster stared at the blue eyes that seemed to shine at him over the top of the black bandanna. They were confident, wise eyes.

'But don't that mean that me being a witness also makes me a target?'

McCall nodded.

'It would if Braddock and his gunmen knew that you were in there when they tortured and killed your boss, son. The thing is, they don't.'

Danny frowned. 'I still don't feel too happy about going back to Medicine Lance.'

'Neither do I.' McCall looked down at the face.

'You mean it's safe for me to return home?'

The Masked Man considered the question carefully. He had already made one big mistake this night and did not want to make another.

'I reckon you'd be safe to go home but I got me a feeling that I ought to try and get you to safety. Just in case.'

Danny watched the tall figure clad entirely in black stepping out into the bright moonlight. The man was thoughtful as he paced around next to his magnificent white stallion.

'I still don't understand what all this is about,' McCall said to Danny. 'Why did they go through all this just to end up killing Eccleston? I can't figure it out.'

'Mr Braddock kept screaming at Mr Eccleston to sign some legal papers he had brought with him,' the youngster told McCall. 'In the end, he did. Then they finished him off.'

'What sort of legal papers were they?' the Masked Man asked.

Danny shrugged.

'Mr Braddock said that they would give him half of my boss's business empire. Whatever that means.'

The Masked Man looked upward. 'Of course. That's it. He wanted to take control of Eccleston's entire company. It must be worth a fortune.'

'But Mr Braddock said he only wanted half.'

'Exactly,' McCall nodded. 'Braddock gets your boss to sign over half the company and when Eccleston is dead, he claims the whole thing. The folks back East won't know that anything's wrong.'

Danny glanced in to the trading post. 'He killed him just to own his company?'

The Masked Man sighed. 'Yep. I'm afraid so. Some folks will do anything to get what they want. It's called greed.'

'How can you stop Mr Braddock?' Danny asked. 'There ain't even any sheriff in town.'

'First I have to get a warrant,' McCall told the frightened youth. 'Then I can act.'

'Is there a place around Medicine Lance that's safe for me to hide out, sir?'

'That's the problem,' the Masked Man said over his shoulder. 'There ain't.'

The young man stepped down into the dust that still showed all the hoof prints of the uninvited dozen or more riders. He moved cautiously to the side of McCall.

'I don't understand.'

'I'll have to take you to Fort Waverley. You'll be safe there and I can get a warrant to arrest Ben Braddock and his men.'

Danny looked at the tall figure.

'You ain't thinking of going up against them alone, are you?'

The Masked Man unwrapped his reins from around the saddle horn. This was one question that he did not wish to dwell on for too long.

'Go and get your horse. We've got a long ride.'

SEVENTEEN

Ben Braddock was like a cat who had discovered a lake of fresh cream. The cattleman knew that the legal document in his hand was worth more than any gold-mine he might have discovered. And it was his alone.

All Braddock had to do was send a message to Eccleston's company headquarters in New York and stake his claim. He knew that he had them tied hand and foot legally. They would have to hand over the entire thing to him and then he would simply clean out their bank accounts and sell off each and every one of the trading posts.

Ben Braddock knew exactly how to get what he wanted. He had proved that fact countless times.

The cattleman had returned to his ranch with half his men whilst Dan Weston

141

resumed his drinking in Medicine Lance with the remaining five gunmen.

'You look mighty happy, boss,' his second-top gun, Joe Slade, had noted as soon as Braddock had triumphantly led the men into the large ranch house.

'I *am* happy, Joe.' Braddock laughed loudly as he waved the papers in the air and made his way to a table which was filled with decanters of whiskey and brandy. 'I just sealed the biggest deal in history.'

Joe Slade had always been an expert marksman with his famed Remington but far more cautious than any of the other men with whom Braddock surrounded himself. He had not ridden on any of the Cheyenne raids with Braddock.

His had always been a more basic job.

One from which he never deviated.

He obediently killed when he was told to kill, but he did not play games. He would not lower himself to dress up in the weathered rags of the Cheyenne, or anyone else, and hound an innocent man as

Braddock had done.

Slade had once been the fastest gun in the West but that was more than a decade earlier. Now he was simply another of Ben Braddock's paid killers.

It had never sat well with the proud Southerner.

'What's wrong with you, Joe?' Braddock asked as he poured himself a beaker full to the brim of whiskey and began sipping it feverishly.

'I take it that you killed Eccleston?' Slade rested his wrist on the grip of his Remington and stared at the man who seemed capable of sinking to depths that even he could not understand.

'Not until he signed this.' Braddock laughed as he waved the paper in the face of the hardened gunslinger. 'We waited long enough for him to put his John Henry down.'

Joe Slade stepped closer to the chuckling man and stared at the shaky signature on the document.

'It's a shame that he got blood on the paper, Ben,' Slade said, raising an eyebrow.

Braddock glanced at the spots of dried blood next to the name of Eccleston and then showed the paper to the rest of his henchmen.

'Looks pretty, don't it, boys? Kinda adds a touch of colour.'

The entire ranch house erupted with laughter. There was not a hint of any of the men regretting anything that they had done to the innocent Jethro Eccleston.

Slade began nodding. He did not stop until he had left the ranch house and filled his lungs with fresh air.

EIGHTEEN

The sun was rising slowly over the vast land that surrounded Medicine Lance. Shafts of golden light spread like wildfire across the tree-covered mountain ranges that flanked both sides of the valley. The sunlight snaked the entire length of the crystal-clear Cheyenne River as it passed through the fertile ranges where thousands of white-faced cattle grazed in blissful ignorance of what was about to happen during the next twenty-four hours.

The Masked Man had ridden continuously for more than three hours since he had left Fort Waverley with the federal warrant tucked in the breast pocket of his black shirt. He had left the youngster named Danny there for his own protection. Even Ben Braddock could not get past 500 cavalry troopers.

But just having the warrant meant nothing and Clu McCall knew it. He had the legal right to arrest Braddock and his henchmen, but he knew that it would take some doing. For men like Braddock did not relinquish their freedom easily. McCall knew that the ruthless cattleman would use every dirty trick in the book to ensure that the warrant was never served.

The Masked Man knew that even he could not simply ride in and round up men such as these. He would have to try and outwit them all, one way or another.

Clu McCall stopped his horse and dismounted.

As Stirrup drank from the ice-cold stream, McCall stared across the wide valley at the mountain opposite, where he knew the Cheyenne lived amid the thousands of tall straight trees. Braddock had used them and now it was his turn, McCall thought.

During the long ride back from Fort Waverley he had come up with the germ of a plan. Something that would create confusion in the twisted mind of the man he sought. McCall knew that it might not work, but there was more than a slim chance that it would shake up the vicious Ben Braddock just long enough for the Masked Man to go into action.

McCall stared over the black bandanna down into the valley below his high vantage point. It appeared so peaceful from where he stood. The truth was far more troubling. He rubbed his eyes.

He was tired, but there was no time to rest.

Quickly he gathered a pile of kindling together and made a crude fire. As the flames began to take, he added more and more dry brush to it until the fire was roaring.

But this fire was not for cooking the breakfast that his belly cried out for.

This fire was for talking with.

The Masked Man untied his trail blanket from behind the saddle cantle and carefully unfolded it.

Then, kneeling down, he draped it over

the fire and held it there for a few moments before releasing the smoke up into the blue morning sky. He had learned long ago how to communicate with the various tribes of Indians that were scattered across the mighty plains.

Long ago, Clu McCall had learned their sign language which he knew enabled nearly all the tribes to talk to each other, as few spoke dialects similar to those even of neighbouring tribes.

Another way of speaking to his red brothers was with smoke signals.

Expertly, McCall fanned the plumes of smoke into the air in a message he knew would be understood by the northern Cheyenne on the mountainside opposite.

When he had sent his short, simple message, he sat down and watched the trees and waited for a reply.

After nearly thirty minutes of waiting beside the small camp-fire, he saw the smoke coming up from between the trees across the valley.

The Masked Man stood to his full height and squinted.

He read the reply.

Without a moment's hesitation, he rolled up his blanket and tied it behind the cantle of his saddle. Then he mounted the white stallion again.

'We got us an appointment with some Cheyenne, Stirrup,' he told the loyal mount as he pulled back on his reins and turned away from the stream.

The Masked Man rode down the steep slope at an incredible pace and headed straight for the opposite mountain range. Within seconds, the tall horse was at full gallop as it thundered across the lush grass.

He knew that countless eyes were watching him from the depths of the dense forest that covered the slopes before him. Eyes that recognized the rider clad entirely in black, who hid his face behind the black bandanna.

But he continued on.

The Masked Man knew that these people might decide to kill him or they might be willing to listen to what he had to say. As his white stallion charged ever onward, he did not pause for one second.

There was not one ounce of fear in him.

For he was the Masked Man.

NINETEEN

There were at least a thousand of them, maybe even more. Clu McCall felt the hair on his neck standing on end as his blue eyes glanced from one Cheyenne face to another. Yet there seemed to be no hostility in their expressions, only a silent confusion.

McCall knew what each of them was thinking as he encouraged Stirrup onward: what was this strange rider with the black bandanna concealing his features doing in the heart of their camp?

The Masked Man began to wonder whether this was indeed an act of sanity or the last act of a suicidal fool. Whichever it was, he could do nothing now but continue riding deeper into the Cheyenne stronghold.

Long before he had caught even a fleeting glimpse of the Cheyenne who now surrounded him, he had heard the rhythmic drumming heralding his arrival into this, their last refuge.

Now McCall could see the elderly men and women beating the hollowed-out tree-trunks and wailing a haunting pitiful cry.

McCall steered the tall white stallion through the trees into the wide clearing and wondered whether this might just be the biggest gamble of his entire life.

Many tribes knew that the Masked Man was a friend to his red brothers, but would the isolated northern Cheyenne have any idea who he was?

His eyes flashed around him as he allowed his horse to walk between the silent, watching people.

The Masked Man had heard tell of the northern Cheyenne but never encountered any before at close hand. He recognized the faces of several of the warriors who had raided Eccleston's trading post two nights earlier. He wondered whether they could see through his disguise and recognize him.

There was a sadness etched in the weathered features of every single one of them. Even the children had the look of people who knew that their very existence and future was probably hopeless.

Once they ruled a territory that stretched hundreds of miles in all directions from this sorrowful place. They had followed the migrating herds of buffalo and lived a life that was in total contrast to the existence they endured now.

McCall tapped the sides of Stirrup again with his spurs and felt the horse respond beneath him.

He could sense an overwhelming sadness emanating from the Cheyenne. These were people who looked nothing like the famed warriors who had fought tooth and nail only a generation earlier against any intruders to their ancient lands.

Now they seemed to be hollow shells.

A broken people who had lost their freedom when the white men had destroyed the nomadic herds of buffalo.

The Masked Man looked down at the young men who had taken hold of Stirrup's bridle. He was no longer doing anything but sitting on his saddle as the braves guided him between the variously sized lodges towards the largest of the permanent structures.

McCall held on to his reins and knew that he was now at the mercy of these people. They could do with him what they liked and he was helpless to stop them.

Yet it was the eyes of the children whom he passed that gave him comfort. They were not the eyes of savages.

The young men who had led his mount to the large wood-built lodge covered in furs released their grip. He watched them walk away as the entire population gathered around him.

McCall stared at the lodge.

Nothing seemed to happen for more than five endless minutes as the rider sat looking at the door opening covered in a massive fur pelt that he could not identify. Whatever the animal had been, he thought, it had been mighty large.

A solitary bead of sweat trickled down from beneath the band of his black Stetson. He did not move a muscle as he felt it travel down his temple and over his cheekbone. All he could think of was the thousands of eyes that were burning into him from the silent people who surrounded his horse.

The drums appeared to be getting louder, as did the continuous wailing from the drummers. McCall still did not feel afraid, but was becoming more and more concerned that he might have bitten off more than he could chew.

Then suddenly the fur door-covering was cast aside and a man dressed in the robes of a chief stepped out before him. The man straightened up. He wore a magnificent war bonnet filled with black eagle-feathers. Its feathered train seemed to almost touch the ground behind him as he stepped closer to the horse. Around his shoulders hung a red blanket covering heavily beaded buckskins.

McCall looked down at the man and

studied him carefully.

There was dignity carved into the face.

The hands of the Indian began to gesture. McCall nodded.

'Yep. I'm known as the Masked Man,' McCall replied to the silent question. 'I reckon that you must be the Chief.'

The Cheyenne stared hard into McCall's face.

'I am called Chief Red Fox, Masked Man. You are known to all my red brothers as a good man.'

Clu McCall dismounted slowly and stepped closer to Red Fox.

'So you do speak English?'

Red Fox touched his own lips. 'When there is someone worthy of talking to, I speak.'

'You flatter me.'

'What does the Masked Man want with Cheyenne?' There was a curiosity in the tone of the voice.

The Masked Man pushed the brim of his hat up off his brow.

'I need your help, Chief.'

Red Fox indicated for McCall to follow him into his lodge. He did. The two men ducked as they stepped into the warm interior of the large structure. A large log-fire burned in the very centre of the round room.

As McCall followed the silent footsteps of the man before him, he gazed around the impressive lodge. It was built of hundreds of straight tree-trunks that had somehow been persuaded to bend high above them. There was a hole in the roof to allow the smoke to escape from the blazing logs that burned in the centre of the floor.

McCall was surprised by the workmanship. The people who had built this were expert carpenters, he mused. Carved benches surrounded them.

Red Fox sat down on one of them and pointed at another. McCall seated himself next to the elegant man.

'You are as brave as stories about you say,' Red Fox said to the man. 'Only the Masked Man would ride into the camp of the

Cheyenne without using his guns to protect himself.'

'I have no reason to use my guns on your people.'

Red Fox stared at the eyes above the black bandanna.

'You were at the trading post with the old man. But you wore no mask that night.'

'How can you tell it was me?'

'You have blue eyes like the sky above. The same eyes.'

McCall nodded.

'You're right. That was me helping Eccleston.'

'You could have killed my braves but did not. You stood before the Cheyenne with empty rifle and were unafraid. The Cheyenne respect that, Masked Man.'

'Like I said, I came here because I need your help,' Clu McCall repeated.

'What help can the Cheyenne give to the Masked Man?'

'I have to capture Ben Braddock. I have legal papers giving me the right to bring him to justice and take him to Fort Waverley to stand trial,' the Masked Man said.

Chief Red Fox glanced away at the flames of the fire and then returned to look hard at the man dressed in black.

'Why do you have to capture Braddock?'

McCall cleared his throat. 'He killed the owner of the trading post.'

There was concern in Red Fox's face. It was clear that he knew nothing of Jethro Eccleston's death.

'When?'

'Last night. He took a dozen of his men to the trading post after dark and tortured the man. He then killed him. The young lad who worked for Eccleston witnessed the whole thing.'

Red Fox stood.

'This is not the way Braddock said it would be. He said that he would not harm the old man at the trading post. We do not wish the blue-coat soldiers coming here to blame us.'

'I know he used your people to frighten

Eccleston, Red Fox,' McCall told the chief. 'I also know that none of your people harmed anyone.'

'My people were hungry. Braddock gave us cattle to feed our children and old ones in return for our help in scaring this man away.' Chief Red Fox brooded. 'I do not understand why Braddock killed him. Why?'

'Because Braddock is greedy.'

'I do not understand, Masked Man.'

'He wanted the things owned by Eccleston.' McCall sighed.

'But what for?' Red Fox asked innocently. 'He has all the land and everything which once was the hunting-ground of the Cheyenne. Why does he need more?'

Clu McCall realized that the northern Cheyenne, like many other tribes, had no understanding of greed. To them it simply made no sense to desire things that belonged to others.

'He is a bad man,' McCall said.

Red Fox nodded.

'We will help the Masked Man.'

TWENTY

It had been Joe Slade who first noticed the afternoon sun dancing off the raised war lances a few miles east of Ben Braddock's ranch house and courtyard buildings. For a few moments he did not quite believe his eyes and walked silently towards the long fence-poles of the large corral near the barn.

The gunfighter stepped up on the bottom pole and climbed to the top of the fence. He continued to squint out at the distant riders who were heading along the bank of the fast-flowing river.

Slowly as his eyes adjusted to the almost blinding light, Joe Slade realized exactly what he was witnessing.

The war bonnet of Red Fox was unmistakable against the backdrop of the tree-covered mountain range. But it was not the sight of the noble chief that troubled the gunfighter, it was the hundreds of warriors riding in single file behind him.

Slade bit his lip and then dropped to the ground.

He felt suddenly frightened. It was an emotion he had not felt in more than two decades.

He turned towards the ranch house and ran. He covered the ground like a man half his age and crashed in through the large doorway.

The sight that met his eyes troubled and disgusted him.

Ben Braddock and the handful of gunmen had been drinking heavily for hours before they eventually collapsed in the chairs that were spread throughout the interior of the huge house.

Joe Slade stopped in his tracks and stared at them.

He was a gunfighter of the old school. He seldom drank hard liquor and had never taken his skills with his weaponry for granted. Yet he knew that none of the other men who were employed to do Braddock's dirty work for him took their jobs as seriously.

Slade knew that none of them would ever live as long as he had. He also knew that none of them deserved to do so.

The angry gunfighter started kicking the boots of the snoring men and shouting at them to wake up.

Gradually he saw heavy eyelids flickering as they emerged from their drunken stupors. Men began to moan and groan all around him but none more so than Ben Braddock himself. The cattleman was still holding on to an empty brandy decanter as he forced himself up from the heavily padded leather chair.

'What you screaming about, Joe?' Braddock asked as he felt the veins in his head starting to thump.

'I think that we have trouble coming, Ben,' Slade shouted.

Braddock dropped the decanter on to the

floor and then used his fingers to massage his temples.

'Hush up. Stop shouting. What sort of trouble?'

'Red Fox is heading here with every one of his warriors.'

Braddock staggered toward the sunlight that cascaded through the open doorway and shielded his eyes. He stared out at the distant Cheyenne riders drunkenly.

'Maybe they want a few more head of cattle, Joe.'

Slade walked up behind the large man and stared at the approaching Indian braves. He knew that they never came down to the open cattle range and never in such numbers. Something was very wrong.

'Red Fox ain't ever come to the ranch before, Ben.'

Braddock rubbed his eyes and tried to rid his blurred vision of the effects of the hard liquor he had consumed after celebrating killing the innocent owner of the trading post.

'Yeah, that's right. They ain't ever come down here before.'

The Cheyenne fanned out in a long line no more than a mile from the compound. The blazing sun glinted off the hundreds of warriors' lances and shields.

'Maybe Red Fox found out that you tried to lay the blame on killing them soldiers on the Cheyenne,' Joe Slade said.

Braddock's expression changed. Every drop of colour instantly drained from his face.

'Go and find out what they want, Joe.'

Slade glanced at the cattleman and then took a deep breath.

'I reckon you must think that I'm as dumb as the rest of your hired guns, Ben. I ain't.'

'I gave you a damn order...' Braddock tried to grab Slade but was no match for the sober gunfighter. He felt the cold barrel of the Remington hitting his jaw. His head jolted backwards as the sound of the gun hammer filled his ears.

'You want some idiot to ask them redskins

what's troubling them, then I suggest that you send out one of your fellow-drunks, Ben,' Slade growled.

Braddock swallowed hard and nodded to the gunman, who seemed to have lost none of his speed on the draw.

'OK, Joe, I'm sorry. You're right. Get one of the boys to go and check out what Red Fox wants.'

Joe Slade spun his pistol on his index finger until it fell neatly back into his holster. He looked at the rest of Braddock's gunmen stumbling around in the room. He knew that none of them would be capable of doing anything until they had poured a few pots of black coffee down their throats.

'You ain't gonna get no joy out of them boys, Ben. Not until they sober up a whole lot.'

Ben Braddock stepped out into the bright sunlight again and forced himself to focus on the Cheyenne warriors.

'What the hell do they want?'

'Blood, by the look of it,' Slade replied. 'I

166

reckon they must have found out about your little deception, Ben. I told you that it was a dumb idea trying to blame them Cheyenne for the killing of those troopers.'

'But how could they have heard about it?'

There was no time for the gunfighter to answer the cattleman. Suddenly the entire wall of Indians let out a combined war cry and thundered towards them. Chief Red Fox rode at the head of the Cheyenne. Their painted ponies tore across the lush range as their screeching masters guided them directly to the ranch house. Cattle scattered in all directions before the unshod horses drove on towards their goal.

Braddock's eyes widened in disbelief.

'What's happening, Joe? What's happening?' the cattleman gasped.

'By the looks of it, we got us some un-invited company, Ben,' Slade answered.

Braddock shouted at his men.

'Get your guns ready, boys. We're under attack.'

TWENTY-ONE

It was the most blood-chilling noise that Joe Slade had heard in all his days. The war cry of the northern Cheyenne could frighten the sturdiest of souls. Arrows showered over the ranch house like rain as the first of the hundreds of Cheyenne drove their ponies at the wooden buildings.

Ben Braddock had somehow managed to find his Winchester and started to fire at their attackers whilst his hired men smashed the glass out of every window in the large house and attempted to fight back.

Only Joe Slade knew that this was no ordinary Indian attack that Red Fox and his followers were waging on the Braddock spread.

His keen, sober mind had noticed that none of the arrows was being aimed directly at any of the gunmen inside or outside the ranch house. Slade gritted his teeth and held his trusty Remington in his hand and pressed his spine against the shadowy wall beside the front door and waited.

The second wave of Cheyenne stormed through the courtyard and released their deadly arrows. They too were way off target.

Slade knew that something was not quite right about this apparent raid. It seemed to the seasoned gunfighter that Red Fox and the rest of the warriors were not actually trying to hit any of them with their lethal projectiles, but guiding them to a place that he had not quite identified yet.

'Let's get out the back way and head for the stables, boys.'

Slade turned his head as he heard Braddock shouting the order to the useless gunmen. His eyes narrowed as he watched the men following the burly cattleman out towards the rear door of the big house.

He was about to move when he saw the third line of riders screaming towards him.

At least fifty arrows hit the wall beside him. The sound of their vibrating was like a thousand angry hornets.

Slade heard the rear door being opened and the sounds of the men firing their rifles and pistols as they fought their way towards the stables, where more than thirty mounts were housed.

It seemed to the gunfighter that Red Fox wanted Braddock to make a break for it but he could not comprehend why. At last, as the fourth wave of Cheyenne stormed past the front of the ranch house, he decided to try and follow the other men.

Slade fired over his shoulder and then ran straight across the large room and out into the empty kitchen area. His high-heeled boots skidded to a halt on the highly polished floorboards.

He forced himself to stop when he saw the bodies lying between the rear door and the large stables.

Joe Slade was now even more confused.

He leaned up against the wall and tried to

make sense of the carnage that lay before him on the blood-soaked dusty ground.

Braddock must have made it to the stables, he concluded, as he quickly identified each of the other dead bodies.

But how?

The Cheyenne drove their ponies around the house in both directions and continued their war cries. Slade bit his lip and wondered again how Ben Braddock could possibly have survived the lethal arrows when his much younger henchmen could not.

How had a man of Braddock's age and size managed to reach the stables, while every one of the gunfighters had been slaughtered?

It was impossible.

There seemed to be no answers, but Slade needed answers real bad. He knew that if the hundreds of warriors were to spot him, he too would be dead meat lying out in the afternoon sun waiting for the buzzards to tear off strips of his flesh before the coyotes came feasting.

Slade looked around carefully. He saw that at least a dozen of the Cheyenne braves had also been cut down from the backs of their mounts and lay scattered around the large area.

Confused, Slade found himself repeating Ben Braddock's earlier question.

'What's happening?' he mumbled under his breath. 'What's going on here?'

Then it dawned on him. The Cheyenne had managed to separate Ben Braddock from his men. For a reason that only they knew, he had to be alone.

Joe Slade caught sight of the flame-faced chestnut galloping away from the back of the stables with the cattleman in the saddle. The gunfighter saw Red Fox pointing at the fleeing rider but not one of the Cheyenne gave chase.

Their mission had been accomplished.

For some reason, Braddock had been spared. The gunfighter began to wonder if there was someone else out there who wanted the cattleman for himself.

Slade found a dark shadow and disappeared into it. He would not reappear until he was certain the Indians had gone.

TWENTY-TWO

Dusk was a time when danger festered unchecked in and around Medicine Lance. The streetlights were being lit as the moon rose slowly into the sky to replace the sun. Respectable females virtually disappeared from sight as the ladies of the night began to fill the saloon, looking for trade.

Of all the men who had been drinking, throughout the long hot day, none had more cash in their pockets than those on Ben Braddock's payroll. They had earned their blood-money and had tried to drown the horrific memories of what it had taken to earn. Yet no amount of hard liquor could wash away the blood that these gunfighters had on their hands.

Only one of their band had never been capable of any feelings of guilt and simply drank because he liked to drink.

Dan Weston had not slept for nearly two days and had continued drinking the town dry of whiskey since his early arrival back at Medicine Lance. His whiskey-soaked mind had blotted out the killing of the Fort Waverley troopers and his part in the torture and ultimate execution of Jethro Eccleston.

Weston had only one thought in his head. He was still celebrating the fact that he had killed the famed Masked Man.

Or at least the mistaken idea that he had managed to achieve that impressive feat.

The rest of Braddock's men had tried to keep pace with the ruthless gunfighter who consumed one bottle of the hard liquor after another, but most had failed dismally.

Weston had left them propped up against the long bar and wandered from the Red Dog saloon reluctantly when he realized that he was hungry. Finding a small café, he had eaten an inch-thick rare steak and then decided to return to continue drinking what was left of the saloon's supplies.

The gunman had managed to walk down the long main street of Medicine Lance without incident. None of the people who dared to be out after dark gave any of Braddock's well-heeled gunmen any trouble, especially the very recognizable Weston.

When he stepped down off the boardwalk to cross the wide street and walk back towards the sound of a tinny piano, which drifted from the open Red Dog doors, he saw an image ahead of him that stopped him dead in his tracks.

Mist drifted between the buildings, making the unmistakable horseman seem almost ghostlike.

The Masked Man had waited for the sun to set before riding into the sprawling township. He rode straight down the main street and then hauled in his reins when he recognized the swaying figure beneath a flickering street-lantern, looking directly at him.

Weston rubbed his mouth and then his eyes.

He could not blink as he focused on the rider of the white stallion clad entirely in black with the famed bandanna pulled up just below his eyes.

The streetlights gave the gunfighter an almost haunting image upon which to try and focus.

Was this the ghost of the Masked Man?

A hundred confused thoughts raced through the liquor-befuddled brain as his hands fumbled for the grips of his guns. With mist drifting through the streets from the mountains, nothing seemed real to the shaking Weston.

Clu McCall wrapped the reins around his wrists and pulled back on them. Stirrup, the mighty stallion reared up and kicked out silently at the air in confident arrogance.

'I killed you!' Weston screamed. He stared hard at McCall through the eerie lights.

The Masked Man steadied the stallion.

'So, it was you who shot at me. I thought so.'

'But I killed you!' the gunman shouted

once more.

'I take a lot of killing,' the Masked Man responded.

'But you fell off the cliff!' Weston growled. 'Nobody could survive that.'

'I did.'

There was no more talking. Dan Weston drew both his guns, but before he could fire them, the mysterious horseman spurred and rode into a dark side-street.

Standing in his stirrups, McCall galloped through the shadows and down the length of the nearest building. He glanced over his shoulder when he heard the shots behind him, then looked ahead.

Forcing the powerful horse on, the Masked Man suddenly saw the overhang of a porch straight in front of him. Without causing his mount to lose one stride, he released the reins and placed both hands on the silver-topped saddle horn. Without a second's hesitation, the Masked Man slipped his boots out from the stirrups and in one swift movement brought both his feet up on top of the saddle. There was no time to doubt his own agility. He began to straighten his legs until he was standing balanced on the wide hand-tooled saddle.

Stirrup galloped on.

As the stallion reached the porch over-hang, McCall threw himself into the air.

His gloved hands found the wooden joist, and he used every ounce of his strength to haul himself upward. Clu McCall grabbed at the whitewashed porch rails and scrambled up on to the high veranda. Before Dan Weston came out shooting, the Masked Man swung around and then crouched down behind the long signboard of the building.

Weston was firing blindly in all directions when he came running through the dust left in the wake of the white stallion's hoofs.

The blue eyes of the Masked Man watched his horse canter to a halt fifty feet away before Dan Weston came rushing out of the dark side-street into the wide dusty yard on to which a dozen buildings backed.

'Where are ya?' he yelled out.

The drunken gunfighter seemed to bounce off the walls of the building in his hurry to catch up with the man whom he thought he had already killed.

Was he chasing a ghost?

The moonlight glinted off the barrels of the drawn pistols as Weston staggered out of the shadows towards the white horse.

'Where are ya?' he yelled again.

There was no answer.

The Masked Man remained silent and exactly where he was. He watched and waited for the moment when he could strike.

Dan Weston was now sweating.

He twisted and turned at every shadow and noise. He could hear the sound of the out-of-tune piano coming from the rear of the Red Dog saloon across the street. Laughter filled the cool night air as it drifted from the open windows and doors.

They were yet more things for the drunken gunman's nervous hands to aim his pistols at.

Weston knew that the Masked Man could

have disappeared into any one of a dozen buildings around him.

But which one?

His thumbs toyed with the hammers of his guns as his eyes darted at every slight sound.

The gunfighter walked to the white stallion's side as it drank from a trough directly below the veranda where its master was crouching. He pressed the back of his right hand against the mount's neck.

It was real!

This was no drunken nightmare, he thought.

The horse was real and that meant that the Masked Man was also real. He was still somehow alive, even though he should have been lying dead at the foot of the cliff on the mountainside. He could hear the sound of a horse galloping ever closer but knew that its rider was not the man he sought.

The noise of the thundering hoofs echoed all around him, making it difficult to work out what was happening in this shadowy place.

Dan Weston rubbed the sweat from his face on to his sleeve and then realized how heavily he was breathing. He was not out of breath and yet he was panting like an old bloodhound.

Was this terror?

He had seen fear in the faces of so many of his victims over the years but never thought he would know what it actually felt like to be totally afraid.

A sudden noise to his left made him swing around.

The gunfighter squeezed the triggers of both his guns and fired into the shadows. The sound of a startled cat rang out around the back of the buildings that faced him.

'Where are you?' Weston screamed out at the black shadows that surrounded him. 'I know that you ain't no ghost. Show yourself, ya yella bastard.'

Clu McCall moved like a puma along the high veranda until he was directly above Weston and the drinking stallion. He placed a hand on the top of the wooden porch rail and was about to leap over it on to the unsuspecting killer, when he too heard the sound of a horse galloping towards town.

Whoever was heading into Medicine Lance made the edgy gunman turn yet again. McCall knew that he dare not continue whilst Dan Weston was so alert.

The Masked Man released his grip on the pole and then ducked down again.

The gunman fired again with both his smoking pistols at the sounds which confused his every sense. Bullets tore through the darkness and bounced off the walls of the buildings.

The sound of Dan Weston's guns finally brought the rest of Braddock's gunmen staggering noisily out into the moonlight from the rear of the Red Dog saloon. They too had their Colts cocked and ready.

When he heard the noise behind him, Dan Weston quickly pulled both hammers back again until they locked. Without thinking, he twisted, turned and fired at the group.

Pitiful whimpers reached his ears as two of

the gunmen fell head first into the dust. They were dead. The remaining men hauled their Colts into the air and aimed them at the man holding his smoking pistols.

Only as the men walked out into the light of the large moon did Weston realize what he had done. But there was no regret in his cruel features, only more anger and frustration.

'You done killed Luke and Frosty, Dan,' one of the men, called Fred Smith, drawled. 'You stupid idiot.'

Weston spat at the bodies.

'Shut the hell up. The Masked Man is around here someplace.'

Smith charged to the side of the snarling Weston.

'I thought you said that you killed the Masked Man, Dan?'

The brooding gunman looked into the angry face. 'I did. Leastways I thought I did.'

'Ya seeing things!' another of Braddock's men yelled. 'Ya just plain loco 'coz ya drunk so much.'

Weston holstered one of his guns, marched

across the distance between them and then grabbed the ear of the man. He dragged him around and pointed the barrel of his gun at the tall white stallion.

'You see that horse? That's his horse. The Masked Man's horse. See it?'

Fearing his ear would be torn from the side of his head the gunman yelped like a wounded pup as his gaze was steered in the direction of the horse.

'I see it, Dan. I see it.'

'I see something else too.' Releasing the ear, Weston had been about to lead the men away when his bloodshot eyes spotted the crouching figure on the veranda opposite. 'Look! There he is, boys. Let him have it.'

The bemused gunfighters followed Weston's lead and began frantically firing up at the crouching man.

Swiftly, the Masked Man drew one of his pistols and started shooting back at Braddock's men below him. The air soon became filled with the acrid stench of gunsmoke. Splinters of wood showered over McCall as bullets tore the porch rail apart.

The Masked Man fanned the hammer of his Colt and watched as one of his bullets found its target. The gunman with the sore ear spun on his heels before falling heavily into the dust.

Weston was still screaming as he unleashed his fury. Bullets tore through the air all around the Masked Man.

McCall knew that he had lost his chance to surprise Dan Weston as his hiding-place was being ripped apart by the gunfighters' bullets. Rolling head over heels to avoid being hit by the lethal volley, the Masked Man landed on his feet and then began to run down the length of the veranda. The night air became alive with red-hot tapers as they passed within inches of his sprinting frame.

Clu McCall knew that he had a decision to make in the next few seconds. Did he stop running or did he try to leap across the gap between the buildings?

There was really only one choice.

He had to jump.

The Masked Man lengthened his stride when he reached the end of the high balcony. His right boot hit the top of the wooden rail and McCall felt himself launch off into the unknown. He threw himself out into the air.

McCall flew across the nine-foot gap towards the smaller structure and landed half-way up its shingle roof.

Catching his breath for a mere second, he glanced over his shoulder at the firing men who were following his every move on the ground.

Wooden shingles shattered all around him as the gunfighters' bullets tried to claim their target.

The Masked Man clawed his way up the roof and then rolled over its top. He slid down the other side and fell off the edge of the building. His boots hit the ground and he found himself in an alley.

There was no time to rest, though. He could hear the spurs of his pursuers getting closer with every breath he took.

The Masked Man got back to his feet, moved to the corner and looked around it.

They were still coming at him with their guns blazing.

McCall fired again and Fred Smith fell lifelessly to the ground at Dan Weston's feet.

The Masked Man looked down the alley and spotted a six-foot-high wooden fence at its end. Without even pausing to think, he holstered his gun and then ran straight at the fence and jumped. His gloved hands caught the top of the fence boards and he pulled himself over.

Before his feet hit the hard ground on the other side he could hear the men entering the alley.

The Masked Man looked around him and spotted a set of wooden stairs leading up to the balcony of the hotel. He raced through the moonlight and mounted the steps two at a time until he was at the top.

Dan Weston was about to clamber over the fence when he saw the figure clad in black darting across the high boardwalk.

'He's on the hotel balcony. He must be trying to get back to his horse. If we cut down Market Street, we can head the critter off.'

Dan Weston and the last two of Ben Braddock's ruthless gunmen ran back up the alley and raced down Market Street towards the side of the hotel.

The Masked Man reached the end of the hotel balcony and was about to head down the staircase to the street when the trio of gasping gunfighters appeared out of the darkness.

Without pausing to regain their breath, they blasted their six-shooters up at the mysterious figure.

McCall felt a sharp pain in his side before he was able to draw his own guns. He fell backwards on to the boards and fired down at the three men who were starting up the wooden steps.

Blood exploded from the first man's chest. He flew backwards knocking his companions down the wooden steps.

The Masked Man rolled over on to his knees and checked his side. He knew that a bullet had skimmed a rib by the blood on his gloved fingers.

Somehow the wounded Clu McCall got back up and defiantly leapt over the rail.

He landed on the ground and then turned with both his guns cocked and ready just as Weston and his stunned cohort managed to clamber out from beneath the dead body. They were barely twenty feet away.

'Kill him!' Dan Weston screamed.

McCall's keen eyes stared over the black bandanna and watched as the two men aimed their guns at him. Then he squeezed his own triggers.

The air between them filled with blinding gunsmoke.

When it cleared, only the Masked Man remained standing. He stared down at the bodies lying in the moonlight. He holstered his guns and touched the arrest warrant in his breast pocket. Ben Braddock was still at large, he thought. If Red Fox had done as instructed the notorious cattleman would have been forced to flee his ranch.

Then the Masked Man heard the sound of a galloping horse behind him.

Turning on his heels he spotted the distinctive chestnut horse pulling up a hundred yards down the street.

'Braddock!' the Masked Man exclaimed.

FINALE

The large yellow moon was still low in the star-studded sky above Clu McCall as he adjusted the black bandanna that concealed his features. He leaned against the wooden staircase that led to the hotel balcony and checked his side again. Blood was running freely from the deep gash that had shattered one of his ribs.

But there was no time to seek medical attention now. For the moment he would have to continue bleeding. The famed Masked Man had to finish the job that he had undertaken only a few days earlier.

His gloved fingers pulled the arrest warrant out of his breast pocket and shook it until it unfolded. He stared at the words illuminated by the light of the moon and then returned the document to the safety of his black shirt-pocket. It was not the first time he had been given the legal right to bring a wanted man to justice, but it was the first time that he had wished he had the right to hang his prey.

Braddock had tortured Jethro Eccleston so mercilessly that the Masked Man knew the cattleman did not deserve to breathe the same air as normal folks.

Braddock's sort had no place in any society, however far from civilization that society might be. But this job had to be done right, McCall thought.

There was no place for emotion now. He had to try to arrest the loathsome Ben Braddock. Without his army of well-paid hired killers to protect him, the Masked Man knew it ought not to take too long or be too difficult.

At least he prayed it would not.

The man in black raised his head and returned his attention to Braddock who was tying his reins to the hitching pole at the rear of the Red Dog saloon. A half-dozen of his men's horses were lined up waiting for the masters who would never return.

Even at the distance of more than a hundred yards it was obvious to the mysterious onlooker that Braddock was in a terrible state. The cattleman continually looked around him as if expecting to see Cheyenne warriors in every shadow. When satisfied that no one had trailed him into Medicine Lance, the wary cattleman rushed inside the saloon.

The Masked Man pulled the brim of his Stetson down and then began the long slow walk towards the now silent building. With every step he took, Stirrup followed at a safe distance from his master.

As the tall lean figure reached the centre of the street he could hear Braddock's raised voice shattering the silence.

But McCall's stride did not falter, even when he stepped over the two bodies lying in the shadows: bodies that Braddock had not even noticed.

There was a steely determination as the

Masked man walked straight towards the line of tethered horses and the wide-open rear door of the Red Dog.

McCall stepped up on to the boardwalk and did not hesitate for even a second. He walked in through the open door with a gun in his left hand as he pressed the glove of his right against the still-bleeding wound in his side.

There was a silence in the saloon which made even the Masked Man slow his pace. There was something evil within the large room that screamed out for McCall to be cautious.

He heeded the feeling and came to a stop at the edge of the stale-smelling room. Cigar smoke still hung on the air in the heart of the saloon.

The keen blue eyes of the Masked Man stared over the top of the raised black bandanna and studied the seemingly empty bar room.

As the tall figure hovered at the very edge of the long saloon room he listened for any tell-tale sign that the man he sought might be lying in wait for him.

McCall could hear nothing except the ticking of the large wall clock as its pendulum swung back and forth. It was like hearing the heartbeat of an invincible enemy. For the Masked Man knew that only time itself could ever be the victor when all men, evil and good alike, were laid to rest.

It was clear that the room had emptied real fast. McCall wondered whether it had been the sound of the gunfight he had just survived which had caused all the saloon's patrons to flee through the still-swinging doors to the front of the building. Or maybe Braddock had frightened them away.

His left thumb pulled back on the hammer of his gun until it locked fully, then he took his next step.

He paced across the stale sawdust towards the long bar and glanced behind it before continuing on. Tables and chairs were on their sides, bearing evidence to the fact that the customers, soiled doves and bartender had fled quickly.

The Masked Man was a mere ten feet from the front of the saloon and about to push through the swing-doors into the main street, when he heard something to his left.

Twisting on his heels, McCall aimed his pistol at the noise that had alerted him. As his gloved finger curled around the trigger of his Colt he saw a female lying on the floor in a corner.

His heart began to beat again when he saw the woman in her low-cut bright-red dress rolling over on to her side. He took a step towards her, thinking that she must just have been drunk or simply knocked over during the stampede that had emptied the Red Dog, when he spotted something.

The eyes of the Masked Man saw that her wrists were tied and her mouth was gagged.

This was no accident, McCall thought.

She had been placed behind the table to distract him.

As he swung around on his heels he saw the blinding flash and then heard the deafening noise of a gun being fired at him from just behind the end of the long bar counter.

The bullet took the black Stetson off his head as McCall instinctively ducked and returned fire.

He saw Braddock's gun being ripped from the cattleman's hand as his own wild shot hit its target. Then he saw the face of the raging man charging at him.

Ben Braddock was no longer young but he still weighed almost twice that of the famed man in black.

Before Clu McCall could rise to steady himself, the burly man crashed into him. It was like being hit by a bull. The impact winded the taller, leaner man as his drawn gun went flying out of his gloved hand.

The Masked Man felt his feet lift off the ground as both men flew backwards. The sound of breaking glass was all around them when they smashed through the large windowpane, fell heavily on to the board-walk and rolled into the street.

Braddock lay beside the stunned, bleeding man in black. He shook the glass fragments from his hair and then grabbed out with both hands.

McCall tried to fight off the heavier man. Both men fought their way back to their feet. Blows landed squarely on Braddock's jaw before at last he released his vicelike grip. The stunned cattleman staggered backwards and then noticed that the main street was now filling with dozens of curious men, women and children.

'I thought you was dead?' Braddock said, spitting out a large lump of blood at the ground between them.

Clu McCall spread his legs apart to balance himself as his bruised eyes spied a rider reining in behind the crowd of onlookers.

'I don't die that easy, Braddock,' he said breathlessly. 'I got a warrant for your arrest and I intend to serve it.'

Ben Braddock growled.

'You better say your prayers, Masked Man.'

'I already done that, mister.'

Both men flexed the fingers of their hands above their remaining pistol-grips and watched each other carefully. There was no room for error now and they both knew it.

Only death waited for the loser of this duel.

'Braddock.' A voice called out.

Both men glanced at the crowd and the rider, who was dismounting. Joe Slade had waited until the Cheyenne braves had ridden away from Braddock's ranch house before setting out after his boss. He pushed his way through the crowd until he was facing the Masked Man with his hand resting on the handle of his prized Remington.

'What you doing here, Joe?' the cattleman asked in a stunned tone. 'I thought them redskins must have gotten you like they did the rest of the boys.'

Slade walked straight towards the two figures, then stopped in front of the man who had paid his wages for more years than either of them could recall. He had put himself between Braddock and McCall.

'You go and get yourself a drink in the saloon, Ben,' Slade said in a voice that had been honed to perfection in many show-downs during his prime. 'This is what you pay me for, ain't it?'

Braddock edged away from the last of his hired gunmen and stepped into the saloon. The crowd began to buzz with excitement as they sensed that blood would soon be spilled.

The Masked Man glared over his bandanna at the man who now faced him. He recalled that Joe Slade had once been faster than any other man alive.

He wondered if he still was.

'I see that them rumours of ya death were a tad premature, Masked Man.' Joe Slade smiled as his hand hovered two inches above the deadly Remington. 'I reckon that I can remedy that, though.'

'If anyone can, I figure it ought to be you, Slade,' McCall responded.

'You know me?' Slade was surprised.

'A long time ago we had us a tussle.'

Slade smiled even wider.

'But you ain't dead.'

'That's only 'coz I'm lucky.' McCall's right hand stayed just above the gun grip, waiting for the exact moment when it would be required to go into action.

Standing just inside the saloon, Ben Braddock pulled his gun from its holster and then cocked its trigger. He pressed his back up against the doorframe and watched the two men squaring up to one another.

Joe Slade could hear the noise of the watching people who had spread to both sides of the wide street, but he did not take his eyes off the man who wore the black bandanna.

McCall's blue eyes burned across the distance between them.

Neither man blinked, for they knew that to blink was to give their opponent a split second in which to draw his gun.

Suddenly, Slade's hand went for his gun. It was a swift move that he had made more than fifty times over the years. But the speed was not what it had once been.

McCall ignored the pain that burned into his side as blood continued to seep from the deep gash. He had waited for Slade to make the first move and now he could see the gun leaving the holster.

That was all the advantage McCall was willing to allow the once-legendary gun-fighter.

The Masked Man drew his Colt, cocked its hammer and squeezed its trigger before the barrel of Slade's Remington had cleared its holster.

The crowd all gave a gasp at exactly the same moment.

There was a stunned expression on Joe Slade's face as he fell heavily backwards. Dust rose from around his body when it hit the ground.

Just as the Masked Man was about to walk towards his fallen victim, someone shouted loudly from the crowd:

'Look out!'

Clu McCall turned his head. He recognized the voice and stopped in his tracks. Before he could see who had called out to him, he felt the heat of a bullet passing by his face an instant before he heard the shot.

Another shot rang out from the crowd.

The Masked Man crouched as his attention was drawn to the saloon. Ben Braddock staggered through the swing-doors and stumbled towards the man in black.

McCall straightened up to his full height when he saw the large red stain covering the front of the cattleman's shirt. The big man dropped his gun and then swayed on the edge of the boardwalk. When the pupils of his eyes disappeared under his heavy lids, Braddock fell like a tree.

The Masked Man felt the ground beneath his feet shake when the heavy body crashed into it.

'Hope you don't mind a little help, son?'

McCall turned his head and suddenly saw the mane of white hair and the trimmed beard of Colonel Zack Walker moving towards him through the shadows. He had never seen the cavalry officer out of uniform before and was surprised by the sight of Walker in a fringed buckskin coat and normal trail gear.

'I don't mind, Zack. Nice to see that you can still hit what you aim at.'

Even in the light of the moon above them, Walker could see that his friend was wounded.

'You're hurt, son.'

McCall strode to the body of the cattleman and turned him over. His gloved hands searched the pockets of the man until they found the legal document. He straightened up and stared at the blood-soaked paper and began tearing it up.

'Are you OK?' Zack Walker asked.

The Masked Man whistled and waited for Stirrup to come galloping out of the shadows. The white stallion slowed to a stop beside his wounded master.

'Are you OK, Masked Man?' Walker repeated.

McCall mounted the tall horse, then tossed the torn-up pieces of paper into the air. He watched the evening breeze take them in all directions before he looked down at his friend.

'I'm fine now, Zack.'

'You need to see a doctor,' Walker said.

'Get your horse, old friend.' McCall nodded. 'I'll let the army surgeon look me over when we get to Fort Waverley.'

Colonel Walker retrieved the black Stetson from the saloon and handed it to McCall. Then he turned, paced through the crowd and untied his horse from the hitching rail outside a small bakery shop.

When Walker turned around to lead his mount back to his friend, all that remained was the dust that had come off the white stallion's hoofs.

The cavalry officer ran his fingers through his long white hair and he began to smile knowingly.

The Masked Man had gone until he was needed again.